THE
BLOODING

BY
PATRICIA WINDSOR

SCHOLASTIC PRESS 🦬 NEW YORK

Copyright © 1996 by Patricia Windsor.

All rights reserved.
Published by Scholastic Press,
a division of Scholastic Inc.,
Publishers since 1920.

Library of Congress Cataloging-in-Publication Data

Windsor, Patricia.
The blooding / by Patricia Windsor.
p. cm.
Summary: While spending the summer working as an au pair
girl for a couple in England, Maris discovers that the husband
is a werewolf intent on blooding her and making her one, too.
ISBN 0-590-43309-1 (alk. paper)
[1. Werewolves—Fiction. 2. England—Fiction.] I. Title.
PZ7.W7245B1 1996
[Fic]—dc20 95-30061
CIP AC

12 11 10 9 8 7 6 5 4 3 2 1   6 7 8 9/9 0 1/0   37

Printed in the U.S.A.
First printing, October 1996

TO MY WOLVES

PROLOGUE

They were found in the woods, curiously and awkwardly lying in the first leaves of autumn. The girl had fallen on top of the man's back; her chin rested on his shoulder. The man's head was twisted slightly, as if he had tried to say some final word to her before he died.

The man had been shot between the eyes, the girl over her right ear. Chief Inspector Hopkins thought it a curious way for the bodies to have fallen.

Both were completely nude and without shoes. There were no clothes in the near vicinity; yet neither were there any signs of a struggle to suggest they had been forcibly disrobed.

"It's odd," said Inspector Hopkins, and Sergeant

Grange, standing next to him, nodded in agreement.

"Perhaps it was some kind of ritual?" the sergeant ventured, having noticed blood and fleshy material on their mouths.

The inspector frowned. He didn't like things like that on his turf. "Let's not jump to conclusions," he said.

The sergeant had further opinions but didn't voice them. He had seen and heard his share of strange things over his long career. When people went out in the woods without their clothes on, you could be sure they were up to no good.

The ambulance took the man away in a black body bag and the girl on a stretcher. Although they pumped oxygen into her and injected drugs to keep her feeble heartbeat ticking, there seemed little hope.

A subsequent search of the area provided little in the way of clues. No clothing, no abandoned car or other means of transport was found. No one had reported seeing a naked couple, and there were no missing persons inquiries. By afternoon, only two items of any note had turned up. One was a dead rabbit with fresh teeth marks, half chewed. The other was an inebriated farmer, who might have been ignored save for the fact that he was waving a gun and shouting that the world was coming to an end.

Sergeant Grange had connections. In forensics, he laid a wager on the teeth marks being human. In ballistics, he put one down for a match of bullets and farmer's rifle. Then he went to the canteen for a cup of tea.

In the Surrey countryside, south of London, an angular old woman was phoning the police. Her face was drawn, its habitual severity even more pronounced.

"The children were left alone," she said, and paused impatiently to listen to what was being said to her from the other end. "The au pair and the father, that's right. They've disappeared."

Behind her, two towheaded children waited.

"I don't like to say what's been going on here," the woman said into the phone. "Although I suspect a thing or two."

The children put their heads together.

"Should we tell?" the little girl whispered.

"Never tell," said the boy.

"But what will we do now?" she asked.

"We have to wait until we grow up," he answered. "Then it will be all right."

"I don't want to wait until I grow up," the girl said.

"You have to," the boy said gravely. "Otherwise they'll kill us."

The old woman put the phone down and turned a baleful eye on the children. "Poor little tykes."

"Who will kill us?" the girl persisted.

The boy glanced at the woman to be sure she couldn't hear.

"Shut up, Vicky," he said to the little girl.

PART ONE

CHAPTER ONE

She had wanted to do it so much, had fought so hard, that even now, as she stood in line waiting for her passport to be stamped, she was afraid she would feel a tap on her shoulder and turn to see her mother, ready to force her to return home.

Of course, nothing like that happened. She was beckoned forward by a man behind a desk; he looked at her passport and landing card; he asked her how long she would be staying.

"Six weeks," she said. "My summer vacation."

He wasn't interested. He stamped a page on the brand-new passport and moved her on with a wave. She had arrived. She was in. Her mother couldn't stop her now.

When she had walked through the corridor labeled NOTHING TO DECLARE, she slipped into the ladies' room and looked at what had been stamped. A *six-month* visa!

If only it were possible to stay that long!

She looked at herself in the mirror and was startled. Her eyes were kind of wild and her hair was a mess from trying to sleep against the window of the plane for six hours. She got out a comb and pulled it through the snarled curls. Then she put some drops in her eyes, the kind that were guaranteed to take the red out. She gathered up her carry-on bags and went out to the luggage claim.

Her suitcases came out almost immediately and she loaded them onto a cart and pushed them out into the reception hall. She looked around at the waiting people. There was a tall woman with pale blond hair holding a sign that said, WELCOME MARIS PELHAM!

"I'm Maris," she said, pushing the cart up to the woman.

The thin, almost sad face that Maris recalled from a blurry photograph broke into a smile and was transformed into a semblance of vitality. "Hello! I'm Mrs. Forrest, but please call me Barb."

They shook hands and Maris felt a little shy. But Mrs. Forrest — Barb — put her at ease.

"Did you have a good trip?" she asked as they made their way to the elevators.

"Terrific. The smoothest ride I've ever had in a plane. And the longest. But it wasn't bad. There was a movie and lots of food and — " She cut herself off, afraid to be babbling. But Mrs. Forrest kept smiling.

"I love your voice," she said to Maris. "I mean your accent. It reminds me of home. Not that I'm homesick, but sometimes I just like hearing a real American voice, not one on TV."

There was an awkward silence as they stood in the descending elevator. The doors opened and they pushed the luggage cart to Barb's car. It was the smallest car Maris had ever seen, like a toy box on wheels. Barb put the suitcases into the backseat. There didn't seem to be a trunk. No, here it would be called a boot. Maris had watched a lot of British TV shows in preparation for this trip. A summer in England. A summer away from her mother.

Barb paid and drove out of the short-term parking lot. When they turned onto the motorway, Maris felt disoriented because they were driving on the left side of the road instead of the right. The gently rolling hills were very green. The trees looked as if they had been specially placed for best effect.

"I love it here," Maris said.

Barb laughed. "You've only been here half an hour. But I know what you mean. It looks so different, doesn't it?" Barb's voice dropped. "There's no mistaking you're not home."

"Don't you like it here?" Maris asked.

"Of course. I've been here ever since I got out of high school and met Derek. Seven years, almost. Feels like forever."

The word *forever* had a plaintive sound. Maris thought Barb must be homesick, whether or not she admitted it. Maris couldn't imagine feeling homesick. She was too excited; she could hardly sit still. But she tried to sit back and relax. She wanted to make a good impression. So far everything was wonderful, just as she had imagined it. Mrs. Forrest was nice. It was going to work out fine.

" . . . it's nothing serious but . . ."

Maris realized Barb had been talking to her.

" . . . it's just so frustrating to have something no one knows how to treat," Barb went on. "They call it TATT here, for Tired All The Time. Sort of like mono. You know, mononucleosis? The kissing disease, I think it used to be called."

Maris laughed. She was going into her senior year in high school and she hadn't done much kissing. But all that seemed far away and unimportant now.

"I'm on a high-vitamin dose and supposed to rest as much as possible. I sleep a lot. But now that you're here, maybe I'll find time to write letters again and keep my journal up to date." Barb looked at her. "I hope you won't find it dull. We don't have many neighbors. It's a typical small English village, very quiet. Your mother did tell you, didn't she?"

Maris nodded.

"Well, we'll soon have everything sorted out and you'll get used to a routine. The kids are not fussy. You're used to children, are you? Your letter said you'd done a lot of babysitting."

"It'll be fine," Maris said lamely, feeling a pang of guilt about the babysitting business. The fact was she had not done much at all. She didn't really feel at ease with kids since that disaster with Jimmy. Anyway, she made more money working evenings for Mrs. Li at the Chinese fast-food place and, even though her feet hurt and her clothes smelled like hot oil, it was easier than trying to entertain kids. Kids always looked at her like she was from outer space. She hoped the Forrest kids wouldn't. Maybe English kids were different. At least that's what she had counted on when she made the big push to get this job.

"You go another country?" Mrs. Li had asked. "You want not stay here anymore?" Her face, usually bright and smiling, had fallen when Maris told her the news.

"Oh, I'm coming back," Maris had said. "It's just for the summer."

"Vacation, okay? Vacation makes big change for you."

"I hope so," Maris had told Mrs. Li.

"Yes, I know. Maybe very big change."

Mrs. Li hadn't been smiling when she said that. But

Maris refused to be daunted. A really big change was just what she needed.

Her last day at work, Mrs. Li gave her a small silk box tied with pale blue ribbon. "You not open now," Mrs. Li had said. "You open on plane."

Mrs. Li was famous for her good-luck charms, so Maris obeyed the instructions. When the plane took off, she untied the bow and opened the box. There was a ball inside. It gave a soft ping when she picked it up from its bed of red satin. The man sitting next to her — from Nigeria, he had said — smiled. "For strength," he told her. "Chinese, right?"

It was a beautiful little ball, painted like a deep blue night sky, with the phases of the moon in delicate ivory and the stars in silver. Maris liked the way it felt in her hand and the sound of its gentle gong. But she was afraid to handle it too much, in case it kept the man from Nigeria awake. He had trouble getting to sleep and turned and twitched until Maris thought she couldn't stand it. But she was sympathetic because he was stuck with an aisle seat while she could lean on the window.

Maris looked at Barb's profile as they left the motorway and turned onto a country road. Her skin was papery and prematurely creased around the mouth and eyes. For a moment, Maris was tempted to give Barb the Chinese ball as a house gift, but Mrs.

Li always said it was bad luck to give your gifts away.

"We'll be there soon," Barb said.

The narrow road snaked through high hedgerows on either side. When a car roared toward them from the opposite direction, Maris's foot pressed the floor like a brake; there seemed to be so little room. But Barb drove confidently. She turned the car into a narrow lane. At its end was a low white house, timbered with dark wood, windowpanes crisscrossed with lead trim in diamond shapes. A thatched roof sat on top like a shaggy head of hair.

"Home, sweet home," Barb said. "Or, more precisely, Sweet Bane. Most houses in England have names."

Bane means something unpleasant, Maris thought, remembering English class, poison or a curse.

"Not very jolly, is it? But that's what it was called when we bought it, and Derek dislikes breaking tradition." Barb began dragging the luggage out of the car. Maris quickly jumped out to help. Two blond children came running across the lawn shouting, "Mummy! Mummy!"

They were shy with Maris and she felt the same. But then the boy took her hand. "Would you like to see my rabbit?"

The ice was broken. Maris was dragged around the back of the house protesting that she had to help their mother, but Barb was delighted. "Go on. Agnes will help me."

A woman stood in the doorway, presumably Agnes. Thin as a skeleton, she could have been anything from sixty to ninety. The little boy, Adam, noticed Maris's glance.

"She's a bit gloomy-acting," he said. The girl, Victoria, straggled along behind, singing a song to herself.

"Isn't Agnes gloomy, Vicky?" Adam asked over his shoulder.

"She is," Vicky agreed, and went on singing.

They turned the corner of the house and were suddenly in the midst of the garden. Maris gasped. "What a beautiful place."

Adam looked around. "It's only the garden."

"Look," Victoria said. She pointed to two birds that had swooped down to alight in one of the flower beds.

"Magpies," Adam told Maris. "Two magpies is good luck. One is bad."

"Don't look if you see only one," Victoria offered.

"It would be hard not to," Maris said with a laugh. "How could you count if you didn't look?"

Victoria's bottom lip came out in a pout. Maris hoped she hadn't hurt her feelings. But Adam was taking over again. "You're right, of course," he told Maris in a confidential tone. "But you can pretend you don't see them. Mummy says it's just as good as not."

"Well, I'm glad there were two this time, anyway," Maris said.

"Me, too," said Adam. He led her to the rabbit hutch

and began fussing with the lock. "We need some good luck around here."

Victoria looked up at Maris and then at her brother. "Do you think she'll be the good luck?"

"I hope I am," Maris said, seriously. And she hoped they would be good luck for her, too. It would be wonderful being part of a family. A real family, with parents and kids. Two people didn't make a family, especially if the people were Maris and her mother.

The rabbit was large and white, with pink eyes and a wiggly nose. Adam pulled him out of the hutch by the ears and gave him to Maris. She stroked him and was delighted when he snuggled up in her arms. Victoria was watching, as if to assess the situation. She nodded to herself, as if Maris had passed a test.

"His name's MacDuff," Adam said. "You must always keep his cage locked."

"Okay," Maris said.

Victoria looked imploringly at her. "Always. Do you promise?"

The two little faces were dead serious. Was there some kind of predator around that attacked rabbits?

"I promise."

She was struck by the way Adam locked the rabbit back in and carefully pocketed the key. A glance passed between him and his sister, a secret sort of glance. As if there were something they didn't want Maris to know.

CHAPTER TWO

Would she ever get used to it? The silence broken only by birdsong, the startling sun on the green lawn, the surging color of the flowers, the twilight that lasted way into the evening and made the days longer and longer than they had ever been.

She didn't want to get used to it. It was still magic. So far, three days of magic. Even gloomy Agnes couldn't ruin it.

Agnes came three mornings a week to do what Barb called the "heavy cleaning." She made cold sandwiches for their supper on Fridays only; otherwise she did not cook, and she never washed dishes. These were her rules and Maris had the distinct impression that they couldn't be changed.

She stretched luxuriously under the cotton comforter. Her room was on the second floor at the back and it overlooked the magnificent garden. The ceiling was low, and little casement windows, with their diamond panes, opened outward. There were no screens and Maris first thought of bugs — there weren't any — and then worried about birds or bats. Barb told her birds soon found their way out. Bats were nothing to worry about. Bats weren't rabid here, Barb told her, so even if they did bite, which was unlikely, there was no need for panic. Maris decided it was a fairy tale and she gave herself up to it completely.

Her job was to mind the children when Barb had to rest. Maris thought maybe she could take over some of the other chores, the cleaning Agnes wouldn't do. It was no effort taking care of the kids; they were always into some project. Maris was surprised at how much she enjoyed being with them. She'd had this idea that kids needed constant watching or they would get into trouble. Or disappear. "Think of the responsibility," her mother had warned. But these kids entertained themselves without any help from her. They were quiet and polite and Maris couldn't imagine them getting into trouble.

It was only eight o'clock but the sun had been up for hours. A murmur of voices came from downstairs. Barb and her husband were probably in the kitchen, talking and drinking coffee before he went to work. He had been a surprise to Maris. She had seen him in that blurred photograph, but he was nothing like that in real life.

That day Maris arrived, Barb had given her a cup of tea and something called a Bakewell tart, which tasted of jam and marzipan and made Maris's teeth ache with its sweetness. She and Barb had been sitting at the kitchen table talking when the car drove up. The children ran out, calling, "Daddy, Daddy."

The slightest shadow had passed over Barb's face, Maris was sure of it. Then Barb smiled and said, "Now you'll meet my husband, Derek."

He was a tall, lean man, with dark hair and dark eyebrows that grew in an almost straight line across his brow. His eyes were a startling combination of honey brown and light gray, fringed with long yet sparse gray lashes. They seemed kind, friendly eyes as they looked upon Maris, so she was taken aback when he turned away and showed a profile of stark severity. The severity remained until he smiled. The change was startling, suddenly tender, yet also mysterious. He shook hands with her. "Nice to have you here, Maris Pelham." His hand was dry and firm, his fingers long and expressive.

"How do you do?" Maris said. She'd taught herself that from watching an old British film with an actress who greeted an entire regiment of soldiers and stopped at each one, saying, slowly and distinctly, "How do you do?" Until then, Maris hadn't known how to meet people. She felt shy and stupid, but if she didn't get some words out fast enough, her mother would say them for her, words that made Maris feel like a two-year-old who couldn't speak for herself.

Barb got her husband out of the kitchen. The children followed. "Let's get dinner on," she said to Maris.

"I haven't been much help, have I?" Maris realized guiltily that Barb had been waiting on her since she arrived. "Why don't you let me take care of dinner?"

It was a rash statement. Maris had never cooked a whole dinner in her life. Her mother wouldn't let her near the kitchen. Too aggravating, she said. Too much trouble to clean up Maris's mistakes.

"Not tonight. When you get used to where stuff is." Barb laughed and gestured helplessly around the cluttered kitchen. "I'll explain how the cooker works and what the kids eat. It's all different from America."

"That's what I like about it," Maris confided. She watched Barb prepare bangers and mash — sausages and mashed potatoes. Everyone ate with knives and forks reversed. Vicky stared and whispered to Adam.

"Never mind, you'll learn," Adam told Maris. His eyes were as honey brown as his father's and could look deeply serious. He obviously had decided to protect Maris.

Maris helped them get ready for bed, but they were self-sufficient children for only four and six. Maris did nothing but stand by as they brushed their teeth and put on pajamas.

They shared a room opposite the one Maris had. Next to each bed was a night-light in the shape of a black Labrador.

"What nice dogs," Maris said.

"These are the only ones we can have," Vicky said.

"Shut up, Vicky," Adam said.

Maris wondered if she should tell them that "shut up" wasn't polite. But they fell asleep almost immediately. Two cherubs. Disturbing cherubs, though. Old souls, Mrs. Li would have called them. "Been around long time before," she often said when she met someone she considered an old soul. "What about me?" Maris had asked.

"You fairly new," Mrs. Li had said. "You get old soon enough."

Now the voices in the kitchen stopped. In a few moments, there would be the sound of the kitchen door closing and the starting of the car. Mr. Forrest would be gone for the day.

Maris realized she had done this every morning: waited until he left for work before getting up. Barb had told her she didn't have to be up at any specific time, that the children liked to visit with their father over breakfast.

What was it that he made her feel? Scrutinized.

Studied. She was aware of his eyes all the time. It made her self-conscious. Like he was waiting for her to slip up, do something stupid. Just the way her mother looked at her, waiting for a mistake to happen.

Barb and the kids were great. Barb talked to her about all kinds of things; she didn't act like she was older and therefore wiser. But Mr. Forrest, he seemed remote. Sometimes he turned his head in a funny way, as if he were listening. Like a dog hearing things people can't hear.

Yeah, right, Maris thought, getting out of bed. It was probably all her imagination. What did she know about men? English men? "The trouble with you, young lady, is that imagination of yours," her mother always said. "The trouble with you is that you're in a dream half the time. The trouble with you . . ."

Maris smacked the pillow and pulled up the bedspread. She yanked on jeans and a T-shirt and took a quick glance in the mirror on her way out of the bedroom. She stopped and looked again. Something seemed different. She looked . . . nicer? There were no frown lines between her eyes. She stood up straighter and pulled her shoulders back and marched downstairs.

Barb was sitting at the kitchen table with a mug of coffee, reading a magazine. She looked up. "Water's hot. Kids are outside. It's a lovely day."

Maris made herself a cup of tea. She noticed Barb's

cup was almost empty. "Can I make you another coffee?"

"Oh, yes, please." Barb put the magazine down. "It's so nice having you here. How is it going so far? Adjusting all right?"

"Fine," Maris said. That was too lame. It was better than fine. It was wonderful to have a conversation in the morning, to actually talk about things like a lovely day and more coffee. Nobody criticizing you the first thing. "It's great," she told Barb. It was like a dream and it was still hard to believe how it all had happened.

Barb's mother and Maris's mother had known each other in college, but they hadn't kept in touch. It was only when Mrs. Pelham read in the alumni magazine that Barb's mother — Dottie Rice — had returned from her daughter's wedding in England that she renewed her friendship by sending a Christmas card. The correspondence continued on and off until Dottie wrote that Barb was ill and looking for someone to help with the kids for the summer. Maris's mother had mentioned it offhandedly. "I could do it," Maris was surprised to hear herself say. Her mother had laughed, then scowled.

"Mrs. Rice's daughter could have something contagious," she said, and when that didn't work, she added, "They want someone responsible, dear. Not someone like you."

It was almost enough. But for once in her life, Maris didn't accept defeat. She turned to the only person she knew who was both sympathetic and powerful: Ms. Epstein, the school counselor. Ms. Epstein didn't give you a lot of garbage; she talked for real. She looked real, too, in jeans or sweats, with her curly hair stuck up on top of her head with binder clips. She drove an old Datsun 280Z and had a dog named Mike who waited outside school for her. When it was bitter cold, the kids sneaked Mike into the basement. Mike had a squinty eye and a snotty look. He was very particular about who he liked.

Ms. Epstein thought England was a good idea. She said she'd ask Mrs. Pelham to come in for a talk.

"What kind of face is that?" she asked when Maris didn't look enthusiastic. "Think positive. Go home and wash some crystals or something."

Somehow, Ms. Epstein prevailed. Mrs. Pelham's arguments fell on deaf ears. "Maris is unrealistic, you know, Miss Epstein. She's a lot like her father. She doesn't think things through."

"She thought this through," Ms. Epstein said.

"What I mean is, she's not very good at sticking to things. And all the way to England! Well!" Mrs. Pelham chuckled. "It won't be a skip and a jump to get back if she decides she doesn't like the job."

"I think Maris will like the job."

Maris had felt like hugging Ms. Epstein. She had

wanted to dance around the office with her. But Ms. Epstein didn't seem excited. She gave Maris a long look and said, "Don't let me down." It was like having ice water thrown at you.

"Maris? You all right?" Barb was asking now. "You looked miles away."

"Just thinking."

"Only good thoughts, I hope?"

"I was thinking how it all worked out . . . my coming here."

Barb smiled and reached for Maris's hand. "I'm glad you came." Maris smiled back, but she felt awkward. Like maybe she was going to cry or something. "Me, too," she said. "I think I better check on the kids."

Adam and Vicky were in the garden, trying to entice a squirrel to eat flower petals.

"Can we go for a walk?" Adam asked.

"Why not?" Maris replied. "Where to?"

"Up in the woods," Adam said. "There are secret places there. We can show you because we've decided."

"Decided what?"

"That you're all right. Didn't we decide, Vicky?"

"We did."

Crazy kids, but you couldn't help liking them. And feeling glad they liked you. "How about a picnic?" she asked.

They thought it was a great idea and Barb thought

so, too. "Agnes will help you put something together."

"I won't," Agnes said abruptly. She was bending down into the cooker oven.

Barb and Maris exchanged glances, and it looked as if Barb was trying not to laugh. Maris made the cheese and tomato sandwiches the way Barb said the kids liked them, with the cheddar cheese grated, not sliced.

"Um . . . we'll probably be going out tonight," Barb said as Maris was about to go out the door carrying the picnic basket. "I'll know when Derek comes home. If we do, I'll leave you emergency numbers."

It sounded as if Barb was apologizing.

"It's okay, I don't mind."

"Thanks," Barb said.

"If you'll get out of my way, please," Agnes said, carrying a basin of ammonia water toward the door.

Maris moved aside and smiled. She wasn't going to let anything spoil the six weeks she was here. Not Agnes, not anyone, certainly not the past. She was capable of babysitting if Barb and her husband went out. In her mind she quickly slammed the door to the place where her mother's voice began to criticize: "You know what happened that one time, Maris. You know it was all your fault."

"I don't," Maris whispered to herself. "But what if I have to stay after school for something?" she said to her mother.

"We'll cross that bridge when we come to it. In the meantime, you start tomorrow. That's if the snow stops and there's school."

Some of the kids thought it was cool for Maris to have a job. They envied her getting five dollars a week just to walk Jimmy Wakefell home from day care. But Maris didn't like it when her friend Sophie wanted to go to the afternoon movie and Maris couldn't get there in time for the show, or when she wanted to go ice-skating and by the time Maris got Jimmy home it was already getting dark and people were leaving the pond. Jimmy was only four and he walked slowly. He stopped all the time and looked at things. Maris only wanted to get him home and she tried to hurry him up. But if she sounded too mean, Jimmy cried and walked even slower. Mrs. Wakefell looked suspicious when Jimmy had tears on his face. Maris had to put up with his snaillike pace.

It wasn't worth the five dollars, even though she had more money than her friends did. It made the winter afternoons seem too long and the dark seem like forever, and finally Sophie got herself a new best friend, one who could go to the early afternoon show or skate before it got dark.

Maris decided if Sophie didn't want to be her friend,

then she'd save her money so she could run away. She'd run away to someplace glamorous and get a real job, not a walking-a-kid-home job. Maybe she'd be a singer in a band. Maybe she'd be an actress on a soap. She'd go to New York and be a waitress while she waited to get a part.

She kept the job until spring and then she wished more than ever that she didn't have to do it. She had thought when it got warmer it would be easier, but instead it was worse. Now she was missing out on a lot more things. She tried to tell her mother that she had to stay for hockey practice, that all the girls did, but her mother phoned the school and said something and the next thing Maris knew, the gym teacher was excusing her from hockey and treating her like some kind of invalid.

She never meant to forget. Picking Jimmy up had become automatic; Maris didn't even think about it anymore. When the last school bell rang, she got her stuff together and walked to the day-care center. She didn't talk to Jimmy anymore and he didn't talk to her. They walked home in silence, hating each other.

But that day it was warm and sunny and Sophie grabbed her arm on the way out and said she'd had a fight with one of her new best friends and she just had to tell someone the news about the gym teacher, who had been caught in the backseat of a car with the guy who ran the gas station.

"You mean the ponytail, tatooed one?"

Sophie nodded.

Maris felt goggle-eyed. The gym teacher seemed far too old and muscular for romance with such an exotic person. Maris stopped to listen to the details. She felt happy that Sophie might be her best friend again. Instead of turning left, which was the way to the day-care center, she turned right and walked home with Sophie. They dawdled and stopped to buy ices from the slush stand.

The moment she saw her mother's face, she remembered. A hollow pit opened in her stomach.

Maris hadn't liked the job or Jimmy, but now she felt scared for him.

"I'll get him right now," she told her mother. "I'll run as fast as I can."

"He's gone," her mother said in a voice that conveyed doom. "He wandered off or something. The teacher thought you had picked him up."

"But — "

"No buts about it, young lady. You're in trouble."

It took two hours before Jimmy was found. He was crying and bruised and nobody really could find out what had happened to him. Nobody wanted to hear Maris's defense: that the day-care teacher was partially responsible.

Maris's mother made her apologize to Jimmy's mother. It was the worst moment of her life. Her knees shook and her voice croaked. Jimmy's mother didn't forgive her. She said Maris could forget that week's pay and not to even think about getting a reference.

Maris thought she wouldn't mind not having the job, but she found she missed the five dollars. Being with Sophie every afternoon wasn't as much fun as she remembered. But worse was the scared panicky feeling that came over her at odd times. It woke her up at night, too, when she had been dreaming about trying to find Jimmy, calling and calling for him through streets that were full of cars and shadows and men in uniforms. After that, every time something got lost or broken, Maris's mother made a comment to remind Maris of what she had done. "You'd lose your head if it wasn't attached," she was fond of saying.

Maris felt like doom would come at any moment. Her neck hurt and she was sure she had an incurable disease, but she said nothing to her mother. Her legs disappeared when she walked on them. Sounds faded and sirens rang in her ears. She thought: *This is what it's like to go crazy.* Only after another whole winter, when she had changed schools for seventh grade, did she feel better.

When Maris later said she wanted the job in England, her mother laughed. "You'll lose them," she said. "Hansel and Gretel all over again."

Maris knew enough to go to Ms. Epstein. She also

knew that Hansel and Gretel were lost on purpose, not because someone had forgotten to pick them up at day care. The woodcutter's wife — their stepmother — had wanted them to die.

"England!" Maris heard over and over again, after Ms. Epstein had fixed it. "You'll be back in a flash. Homesick in a week, mark my words. Remember when you went to that summer jamboree? Couldn't last a day! Crying on the phone to come home. And I had to cancel my trip to Florida."

"I was sick," Maris said. "I got the chicken pox, remember?"

Her mother ignored this information. She was good at doing that. "You'll be crying to come back before you know it."

I won't get chicken pox this time, Maris thought. Get it once and you're immune. Nothing in this whole world would make me say I wanted to come back. Not until I'm good and ready.

CHAPTER FOUR

M aris heard them come in. It seemed very late. She started awake guiltily, wondering if it had been wrong to fall asleep. Even though Barb had told her to do just that, Maris had kept her jeans on and lay on top of the bedspread, just in case of an emergency. There had been no problems at all and she didn't have to phone the people down the road whose number Barb had given her.

Barb had told her, "Just leave the porch light on and go up to bed when you're ready. The children know to call you if they need you. You're right across the hall."

Maris looked at her watch and was astonished it was nearly four A.M. Barb had said they would only go to a pub and have a meal. Maris felt upset that she hadn't been told they would be out so late. What if she had awakened earlier and thought something had happened?

"Shut up, Maris," she told herself, imitating Adam. Mr. and Mrs. Forrest had a perfect right to stay out all night if they wanted to. And nothing had happened, had it?

She quietly took off her jeans and crawled under the covers, not wanting Barb to know she was still awake. She could hear them talking to each other downstairs and it somehow sounded like an argument. It made her feel funny inside, to hear them argue. She wanted to listen closely to be sure, but she didn't want them to think she was spying.

She was almost asleep when she heard them come up the creaky stairs. One of them went into the bedroom and the other into the bathroom. The water began running in the cistern above Maris's room. She was drifting off to sleep again when suddenly there was another sound. Gagging. Vomiting.

It went on a long time. Or maybe it just seemed long because Maris had to listen. Finally there was the sound of flushing. And then water running in the sink. Gargling! She put the pillow over her head. She didn't want to imagine Barb or Derek Forrest being sick, maybe because of drinking too much. It was embarrassing.

Why was it that she always felt responsible when

things like this happened, as if it were her fault? When Sophie fell out of a tree they were climbing to stick a freshman flag at the top, Maris cried more than Sophie did because it had been her idea.

"What's with all your guilt?" Ms. Epstein had asked. "Sophie fell by herself, without any help from you."

"Why you carry world on your head?" Mrs. Li once said. "Plenty other heads to go around."

Maris smiled, remembering. In a funny way, Barb sort of reminded her of Mrs. Li. It had nothing to do with being Chinese. More about being calm. Mrs. Li and Ms. Epstein were right. It wasn't her fault if the Forrests drank too much and got sick. It was their problem.

CHAPTER FIVE

Adam and Victoria woke Maris the next morning. They came into her bedroom and jumped on her bed, snuggled next to her. Awkwardly, Maris put her arms around them. They smelled of some special little kid smell, shampoo and sticky candy and crayons.

"Mummy and Daddy are having a lie-in," Vicky said.

"We're not supposed to make any noise," said Adam.

Maris looked at her watch, surprised to see that it was already past nine. "Have you two been awake long?"

Vicky nodded. "We stayed in our beds and colored pictures."

"Mummy and Daddy feel under the weather," Adam said.

"Mummy says under the weather," Vicky corrected. "Daddy says knackered."

"Let's do something," Adam said.

"What do you usually do on Saturday?" Maris asked.

"We go to the market if it's first Saturday. But it's not, so we can do whatever we like."

Maris had a sudden desire to be among the bustle of people, to look in store windows and hear the noise of traffic.

"Let's walk to town."

They looked at her as if she were crazy.

"There is a town, isn't there?"

"It's far away," Vicky said.

But Adam recognized her disappointment and said, "There's a bus."

"Good. Then we'll take it."

Adam assessed the situation. "We'll have to wait for the afternoon one. I'll feed MacDuff and you can make us breakfast."

Maris laughed. That was what she was here for. Maybe this was a good opportunity to do a little more than she had been doing. The light cleaning, if the Forrests were under the weather or knackered.

"We'll have brunch," she told them. "That's a combination of breakfast and lunch. And then we'll go to town."

She tiptoed into the bathroom to see if there was any hot water. Sometimes the boiler ran out. She had learned not to count on washing her hair every morning as she did at home.

There was enough for a steamy bath. The Forrests didn't have a shower, only a sprayer attached to the faucet that you could hold over your head.

She got into the bath quickly; even though it was summer, the bathroom was cold. She used some of Barb's bath salts, but she could only luxuriate a few minutes. The kids were waiting for breakfast.

When she had dried herself, she gave the bath a quick sponging. Then, because it was easy enough to do while she was in the room, she sponged out the sink, cleaned off the mirror, and wiped the faucets until they shone. Under the sink she found a bottle of toilet cleaner. On a roll, she picked up the lid and seat to squirt it in, remembering also last night's vomiting. She felt squeamish for a moment. Maybe it was too forward to be cleaning the toilet after that. Would it look like she had heard and disapproved? Oh, shut up, she told herself, and reached for the toilet brush.

There was some stuff under the rim. She really didn't want to look. But when she swished the brush in the bowl, she couldn't help noticing that the water turned red. This was really beyond the call of duty. She gave the brush a shake. Something clung to the bristles. A chunk of something pinkish, like a piece of raw meat. A piece of steak, somebody's dinner? Oh, God, why had she started this stupid cleaning? She gave the brush a furious shake and at last the thing disappeared down the pipe when she flushed.

That was it, enough. She stuck the brush back, put the cleaner under the sink, and washed her hands. One of the hand towels was dirty — muddy, in fact, probably from the kids. She opened the hamper to sling it in and saw a wet washcloth on top of the pile, seeping red stuff into the rest of the dirty clothes. Train wreck, she thought, slamming the lid and feeling annoyed. She didn't want to see the Forrests' private messes.

The kids were in the kitchen, banging crockery. Setting the table was their regular job, but they were making too much noise. If they got the Forrests up, Maris would have to look them in the eye, trying to forget steak in the toilet and pizza in the hamper.

She hurried downstairs. The table was set with an eggcup at each place. Vicky was pulling rashers of bacon apart, her tongue stuck between her teeth in concentration.

"We helped," Adam said, sitting down in his chair as if to say that now that Maris was there, no more help was needed.

Maris looked at the eggcups with dismay. She had planned to make scrambled eggs, something she knew how to do. She didn't know how to boil an egg, which was like a joke — people said that about people who couldn't cook: She can't boil an egg.

"How many minutes do you like your eggs?" she asked in a fit of brilliance.

"Half soft," Vicky said, having arranged the bacon on the grill.

"How long does that take?"

"How would I know?" Vicky said.

Adam looked at her suspiciously. "Don't you know?"

"Well. Well, the truth is, I don't. I've never boiled an egg."

They gaped at her.

"Well, except hard-boiled."

"Do you know how to do anything?" Vicky asked.

"Scrambled? Would you like scrambled for a change?"

"Of course," Adam said, mollifying the situation as usual.

It turned out to be a nice breakfast. She got the kids to help turn the bacon and suggested that Adam cut some tomatoes and put them under the grill. She made the toast and put the slices in the rack and stuck it on the table with a flourish; but Vicky gave her a look that said, *Anyone can make toast.*

Afterward, they did the dishes together. Adam dropped the spoons and Vicky almost smashed a cup, but Maris didn't scold them. She wasn't going to act like her mother.

She realized it was almost noon. Still no movement from upstairs.

"What time does the bus go to town?" she asked.

They looked blank — until Adam brightened and opened a cupboard door. "Mum has a schedule tacked in here."

Maris looked helplessly at the numbers. The times were written in what she once learned was a military way. 14.25. 16.25. She counted on her fingers. Did fourteen mean two o'clock? Wasn't there one sooner?

She remembered there was a footpath along the road. Barb had pointed it out. "I used to jog on that, if you can imagine," she had said in a sad sort of way.

"You know what? Let's see how far we can walk. It's a beautiful day."

"Walk *all* the way?" Vicky asked doubtfully.

"We'll start out walking. If we get tired, we'll wait for the bus."

She was relieved when they agreed. She had heard a stirring above. She had a sudden urge to get out of the house as fast as she could.

CHAPTER SIX

They went over a stile to get to the footpath. Maris was enchanted. She'd only read about stiles in stories. There were wooden markers, pointing to the names of villages. Adam had explained that they were villages, not towns. A town was a big place, with traffic and buses and noise. A village was what they were going to, their village, called Banfield. The path ran alongside the split-rail fence, separating walkers from the road. To the other side lay bright green fields, recently cut grass lying in little piles, making the field look like a sea topped with gentle whitecaps.

Birds sang in the trees, one of them sounding like the neighing of a horse. Blackbirds swooped.

"Lovely, isn't it?" an old woman with bright eyes

and red cheeks said as she passed them. Her dog ran up the slope and back again, a large stick in his mouth.

There were other walkers with dogs, letting them run up and down, getting exercise. The dogs seemed singularly well-behaved, to Maris. They stayed with their owners and didn't come up to say hello the way American dogs had a habit of doing. Adam stopped once or twice to watch. Longingly, Maris thought.

"Would you like to have a dog?" she asked.

Adam shrugged.

"It looks like everybody has dogs around here." She recalled the conversation about the night-lights in the shape of dogs — the only ones they had, as Vicky had said.

"Are you allergic?"

"We had a dog," Adam said. "Dad didn't like him."

"You've got it wrong, Adam," Vicky said. "He didn't like Dad."

Adam turned on her, his face angry. Maris quickly stepped in. "Sometimes dogs are like that. You can never tell."

"Do you have a dog, then?" Vicky asked.

"No, I don't."

"Arc you allergic?"

"No, my mother doesn't like animals. They dirty up the house, she says. Of course, we don't live in the country like you do. A dog would have to stay indoors a lot."

Adam still looked uncomfortable. Maris quickly changed the subject. They talked about what they would do when they got to the village. Adam and Vicky wanted to buy candy. Sweets, they called them.

They didn't think about the bus. The children didn't complain about the distance and neither did Maris, although it was probably one of the longest walks she'd ever taken in her life. Well, they could take the bus back.

As soon as they rounded the bend and saw the shops, Maris realized what Adam meant about the difference between a village and a town. Banfield was simply two rows of shops, up and down a little hill. Banfield Parade, it was called. A circular red and yellow POST OFFICE sign hung from a store that looked more like a grocery than a post office. It was there Adam said they would buy their sweets. Inside was a jumble of newspapers, magazines, stationery, and a massive display of candy. On the shelves behind the counter were odd bottles of aspirin, laxatives, and cough syrups. The post office was simply a small counter to the side with a grille in front of it.

Maris thought she should buy some postcards to send home. Her mother would be expecting one. And Sophie. Maybe she should buy a newspaper, too. The world seemed remote, news far away. She looked at the newspapers and didn't recognize any of them. Some looked exactly like the supermarket rags, the ones that had nothing but trashy stories in them. She couldn't recall if the Forrests had any newspapers since she'd been there.

Adam had been watching her, clutching his candy bars.

"Buy the *Sun*," he advised.

Maris did. But as they waited for the bus and she glanced through it, she saw the *Sun* was full of nothing but scandals, stories about the royal family having affairs, and people being murdered. Adam wanted to read it, but she wouldn't let him. She had a feeling he had tricked her into buying it. "Later," she said. "I'm still reading this story."

Adam and Vicky crunched their candy bars. Maris read about a woman who had poisoned three husbands. She turned the page and read her horoscope. "Stop soul-searching and agonizing about the future," it said. "Nothing of significance will happen for at least a few days." Next to the horoscope was an advice-to-the-lovelorn column, full of sordid problems.

And then, just before pages and pages of sports news, there was a headline that caught her eye because it was about dogs. Dogs had been suspected, it said, in the brutal attack on some cattle the month before. Because the local authorities had done nothing about finding the dogs, the farmer whose cattle had been killed had shot a neighboring farmer's Alsatian. There was a picture of a big German shepherd, with his tongue hanging out, looking as if he were laughing. "Laddie," it said underneath. There was a separate story about Laddie's owner and how heartbroken he was. "Laddie would never do a thing like that," the owner was quoted, referring to the dead cattle.

Maris had read similar stories in American newspapers, usually while she was standing on line at the drugstore. Aliens were often suspected in the cases of mutilated cattle. She was sorry for Laddie. In his picture, he looked very kind-hearted.

They got off the bus at the end of the long lane that led to the Forrests' house. There was a house on the corner of the main road, near the bus stop, its front garden neatly lined with flowers. A sign on the gate read MILESTONES. Maris realized that the people whose number Barb had given her the night before lived here. They seemed to be the closest neighbors. A large tabby was curled comfortably on the front doormat, sleeping in the sun.

"What about a cat?" Maris asked absentmindedly.

"What about a cat?" Adam asked.

"If you can't have a dog, maybe you could have a cat."

"We don't need a cat," Vicky said. "We've got MacDuff." Maris didn't pursue it.

When they got to the cottage, Mr. Forrest was sitting in the garden, basking in the sun much in the way the cat on the doorstep at Milestones had been. He gave Maris a smile of such brilliance that she wondered if the sun had caught her in the eye or if she was seeing him for the first time. He looked suntanned and incredibly healthy, and his eyes sparkled in a way they had not done since Maris had arrived. He beamed at her, at the children; he asked them questions about their walk, about whether they had shown Maris the village; he gently rebuked them for tricking her into letting them buy so much candy.

"Gosh, I'm sorry," Maris said.

"Don't be silly," he replied. "Wouldn't you do the same in their shoes?"

He smiled again and the sun seemed warmer. Maris felt herself blushing. She had not realized how attractive he was.

"Where's Barb?" she blurted, afraid he would notice she was staring.

"She's not feeling well. Why don't you take her some tea?"

So it had been Barb who had been sick last night.

"Of course I will."

"Thank you, Maris. It's a real help having you here."

It was the nicest thing he had said to her so far. Maybe it hadn't been fair, not liking him before.

He began to play with the children, running in and out of the shrubs, hiding and jumping out at them. They laughed and screamed in delighted terror. But as

Maris was filling the kettle at the sink under the kitchen window, she thought that maybe Vicky's laughter sounded too hysterical. That Adam's shrieks were of real terror. Was it good for kids to get so excited? How little she knew about them. She wished she knew more so that she could really help. But she'd do the best she could. Barb trusted her and had given her a chance.

She could hear Barb coughing as she carried the tea tray up the stairs. She had tried hard to make things look appetizing, cutting the toast into triangles, putting jam and marmalade into little dishes, putting the milk into a pitcher. It was the kind of thing she always wished she could have when she was sick in bed.

Maris felt proud and apprehensive at the same time. She hoped Barb wasn't too sick. She had never thought about coping with real illness. Her mother's words came back to her. Something contagious.

She balanced the tray against the hall table and knocked on the bedroom door.

"Is that you, Maris? Come on in."

Barb was sitting up in bed, a shawl around her thin shoulders. Her hair hung lank around her face. The room was musty and dark and smelled odd. Maris put the tray down and went over to pull back the drapes. Sunlight streamed in. The children's laughter rose up from the garden. Maris turned around and was shocked. Barb's skin was almost transparent, as if you could see the bluish veins beneath it and the bones pressing against the taut flesh. Her eyes were sunken but bright. Too bright. She must have a fever. She gave Maris a wan smile. "Thanks. Everything looks so pretty." She poured out the tea and drank almost greedily. "I had a bad night. But I'll get up soon."

"Shouldn't you stay in bed?"

"Oh, no, I have to get up. It makes Derek angry if I lie in bed all day."

"But you're sick." Maris didn't understand. Mr. Forrest had seemed concerned, not angry.

"I'll be fine, really. Just give me a few more minutes."

"Should I take something out of the freezer for dinner?" Maris asked.

"There's . . . some . . . chicken . . ." Barb turned away. Maris could see her neck working, as if she were trying to hide herself gagging.

"Take the chicken out," she said, and leaned over to pull a tissue from a box next to the bed. A pile of used, crumpled tissues lay helter-skelter on the floor. Some of them, Maris was sure of it, were tinged with red.

Barb covered her mouth. Her bright eyes caught Maris's eyes and held for a second. They were wide and desperate. This frightened Maris. She was glad to get out of the bedroom. She went down to the little room off the kitchen that Barb called the larder. In it was a big freezer, to supplement the small refrigerator in the kitchen. Maris had been astonished that a family of four could manage with the kind of fridge that Americans used only in offices and motel rooms. The freezer helped cut down on shopping; Barb didn't always feel well enough to go into town.

Maris took the package of chicken out and put it in the refrigerator. She'd defrost it later, in the microwave. She looked out from the kitchen window into the garden, where Mr. Forrest was still playing with his children. Adam caught her watching them and gave her a smile. But Maris couldn't help thinking that his eyes were exactly like his mother's. Bright and desperate. As if he were only pretending everything was okay.

CHAPTER SEVEN

Dinner was a disaster. Barb made an effort to appear well, but she obviously wasn't up to it. Maris didn't see why she refused to go back to bed. If she was sick, she was sick; why pretend otherwise?

What made it even worse was the way Mr. Forrest acted. He made remarks about Barb, as if she weren't even there. Or he was polite in an exaggerated way, saying "Why, of course, my dear," when she asked for the salt, and "You certainly may have more bread, darling." It wasn't so much the words as the way he said them. Once he caught Maris's eye and winked. She acted as if she hadn't noticed. She knew Barb was upset and trying to hide it.

Adam was bothered, too. He kept his eyes fastened

on his plate and pretended to eat with great concentration when he was only pushing his food around.

Only Vicky was unaffected. She stuffed roast chicken and mashed potatoes into her mouth and chewed with satisfaction. When her plate was clean, she sat back and said, "I was that hungry I could eat a scabby horse!"

Adam looked shocked and Barb raised her eyebrows and said, "Vicky, dear, *famished* is a better way of saying it."

But Mr. Forrest laughed. He said Barb was making a face like a mackerel. Vicky laughed, too, and Adam tried to cover up a smile.

Barb was furious. She threw her fork down. "That is absolutely not funny, Derek," she said. "And it completely undermines my authority."

"Your authority?" Mr. Forrest said. There was an icy sarcasm in his voice. Maris wished she could crawl under the table.

There was a moment of complete silence. Adam's face had turned red. Vicky seem bewildered, not knowing whether to keep laughing or become silent. Mr. Forrest looked impassively at Barb.

"Excuse me," she said. "I'm not well. I should have stayed upstairs."

She pushed her chair back and got up from the table. She placed her knife and fork on her plate and was about to carry it to the sink. Maris wanted to cry out

It's okay, I'll do it! but she was too embarrassed. It was Mr. Forrest who said it, his voice gentle this time. "Yes, darling, you should have stayed in bed today."

"Yes." Barb made a sound that was either a giggle or a sob. She left the kitchen quickly.

"It's all right, Mum's feeling poorly," Mr. Forrest said to the children. "Sorry about that, Maris."

"It's . . . it's okay. I mean, I know about Mrs. Forrest." He gave her a piercing look. "I mean, that's why I came — to help out," she added lamely. What was he staring at her for? What had she done?

They finished the meal in silence. It was awful, Maris thought. Nobody really wanted to eat, but they kept doggedly pushing food around as if they hoped it would disappear. Even Vicky was subdued, although she perked up when her father asked if she wanted lemon meringue pie.

"Yes, please!"

"There isn't any," Adam said.

Mr. Forrest looked around, as if expecting the pie to appear out of thin air.

"I guess I forgot to take it out of the freezer," Maris apologized, feeling protective of Barb.

"I'm sure it's not your fault," Mr. Forrest said.

"Oh, it is, I'm sorry." Maris wouldn't let him think Barb had forgotten to instruct her. Take the chicken out was all she had managed to say before she started gagging. But he didn't have to know that. Maris was getting a new perspective on Mr. Forrest. He could be a tyrant. And he could be mean. Maybe that was why Barb was sick. Men could make you sick; isn't that what her mother was always telling her?

Maris had never wanted to believe her mother — not about anything. But the words rang in her memory, hard to dismiss. "Men, men, men," her mother was always saying. "Let you down every time."

Finally Mr. Forrest decided the meal was over. "Let's give Maris a hand with the washing up," he said.

"Oh, no, I'll do it," Maris said, wanting to be out of his way. But she sensed disapproval. "I mean, Adam and Vicky and me . . . we'll do it together. You don't have to be bothered."

He smiled at her. The brilliant smile again, darkened only slightly by the indoor light. "It's still lovely outside," he said. "What do you say? Will we all go for a walk when the washing up is done?"

Adam and Vicky shouted yes. Maris thought she should say she would stay and keep Barb company. It was only right that someone should be there in case she needed something. Mr. Forrest seemed so callous.

As if reading her thoughts, he said quietly, "It's tiring when someone is ill. That doesn't mean you don't care."

Maris felt her face go crimson. She turned away and began collecting the plates. She took them to the sink and turned on the water and squirted washing-up liquid into the dishpan. With a great effort, she found her courage and her voice. "Adam, you dry," she said. "Vicky, you put the knives and forks away."

"Forks, corks, knives, hives," Vicky chanted, waiting by the sink happily until some clean silverware appeared. She put them very carefully into the correct spaces in the kitchen drawer.

Maris didn't know if Mr. Forrest was still in the kitchen or not. She had a feeling of being watched and it made her very self-conscious. But she refused to turn around and look. When she did, when it was a natural moment to do so, she discovered he wasn't there at all.

She really didn't want to go for a walk, be with him, even if the kids were there. She'd had one of the longest walks in her life already that afternoon. Could she just say she was tired?

No, she couldn't. Not when Adam took her hand so shyly and pulled her. He wanted her to come. She and Adam had something in common, she thought with sudden clarity. Adam was a little afraid of Derek too.

"Wait," Maris said, collecting scraps from the garbage. "Did you feed MacDuff?"

"We'll do it later," Adam said.

"Daddy's waiting," Vicky said.

It was stupid, but Maris got a cold feeling of dread as she went out into the garden with the children. But there was Mr. Forrest, leaning over a flower bed, pulling out weeds. He straightened up and dusted his hands off on his trouser legs. Then he swung Vicky up over his shoulder and carried her along, singing some song. Vicky giggled and sang along. It was all so normal, so charming, Maris could almost have chided herself for being afraid. Only Adam's hot little hand, holding hers so tightly, gave her a clue that her fears might not all be imaginary.

"Who's afraid of the big bad wolf?" Mr. Forrest sang.

" . . . the big bad wolf, the big bad wolf," Vicky sang along.

They walked in the opposite direction of Banfield, away from the footpath Maris and the kids had taken that afternoon. They entered the woods that Adam had said were all right in the daylight when they went for a walk the day before. It was going to be evening, even dark soon. Was that all right? Mr. Forrest stopped singing and turned to Maris. His arms hugged Vicky's legs around his shoulders as he looked down. "No wolves allowed in these woods," he said. "Wolfless woods." He laughed. Vicky began to sing again.

Maris felt alarmed. "Are there wolves here?" she asked. "I thought they were extinct."

"They stink!" Vicky shrieked, and laughed, pounding her father's head with her fists.

"Only foxes," Adam answered quietly.

"Do you like foxes, Maris?" Mr. Forrest asked.

"I've never seen one. I mean, I've never seen one for real."

"They won't hurt you, you know," he went on. "They're growing very tame, getting used to people, even though they get hunted down by the blood-sporters. They don't learn. Do you know what they do to you the first time you go fox hunting?" He shifted Vicky more comfortably on his shoulders, oblivious to her pulling of his hair. "They blood you."

"What's that?" Maris asked.

"Take some of the dead fox's blood and smear it on your face."

Maris glanced nervously at Adam.

"Don't worry, he knows all of it," Mr. Forrest said. "It's a tradition. It probably seems barbaric to you. But Americans have barbaric traditions of their own."

Why were they talking about this? Maris thought. Was he trying to scare her? She wished he'd stop. Vicky was oblivious, but Adam didn't seem too happy. He still clutched her hand. She stepped ahead purposefully, asking Adam the names of wildflowers. She wasn't going to be bullied. Behind her, Mr. Forrest and Vicky kept on singing about the big bad wolf. Finally Adam relaxed and let go of her hand. Mr. Forrest began to talk like a normal person, asking Adam about his summer homework and whether or not he had been seeing his school friends.

"Clive went to the seashore," Adam said. "I don't

have any others." His little-boy's voice was plaintive, and Maris had a sudden sense of his loneliness.

His answer seemed to subdue his father. They continued quietly, until they were deep into the woods, farther than she and the children had gone on their picnic. The landscape seemed manicured, as if every tree had been set carefully into its spot and every tangle of underbrush or canopy of shrubs had been placed on purpose, as if it were the set of a play. It all began to seem unreal and Maris had the feeling that at any moment something weird would happen: A fox would appear, wearing a hat and waistcoast, or a wolf would want to know if they had seen Little Red Riding Hood. She began not to like the woods, to feel as if something were watching from behind every tree. The fox and wolf would walk on their hind legs, would turn their feral faces toward Maris and grin.

"All right, Maris?" Mr. Forrest asked.

"Fine," she said, snapping herself out of it. The path wound around a circle of fir trees, turned back on itself, and pointed them toward home.

The evening was fading. As they neared the house, the lights from the windows twinkled through the trees like a beacon. Vicky was restless now; she wanted to be put down. Adam raced ahead.

"Mummy," he cried. "Mummy!"

Vicky followed suit. The children disappeared into the house through the kitchen door.

Maris felt uneasy alone with Mr. Forrest. She had a mad desire to run after the children, screaming "Mummy!" herself.

Mr. Forrest sighed. "That's right," he said, looking after his children. "Go to your mummy."

It sounded so bitter, she had to look at him. But his expression was nothing like she expected. It had a forlorn look, a yearning that gave the handsomeness even finer structure. She almost said something. She wanted to comfort him. But he didn't even glance at her as he walked through the garden to the house. He seemed to have forgotten she was there.

CHAPTER EIGHT

On Sunday night Mr. Forrest went out alone. He must have told Barb at some point in the afternoon that he was going because Maris heard them beginning to have an argument.

Maris and the kids were on the lawn, playing with MacDuff. Maris thought the rabbit would certainly run off if it was let loose, but it seemed tame enough to stay with them, even come when Adam called to it. Maris had brought down her Chinese ball, the one Mrs. Li had given her, and MacDuff could be coaxed into chasing it. The nearest thing to a dog they would get, she supposed. The angry voices drifted out from the house, rising in volume, and it was impossible to ignore them. But as suddenly as they started, they stopped, as if Barb and her husband realized they could be overheard.

Maris's heart sank. She had managed to get through yesterday, get the kids to bed and herself to sleep. This morning things seemed much better. Barb was up bright and early, looking more normal, although for her, normal was a wan face and tired eyes. Still, she made them all breakfast for a treat, insisting that Maris be served. She's making it up to me, Maris thought. She feels embarrassed about yesterday. Maris promised herself she'd do everything she could to put Barb's mind at ease. She wondered if Barb was worried that she might want to go home.

But now here was another argument starting and what had seemed like a great job was fast becoming a nightmare. Was it going to be like this every weekend? Thank goodness Mr. Forrest went off to work on week-day mornings.

Why did Barb put up with it? Why didn't she go home, back to the United States? Why live with arguments?

Maris was ready to take Barb's side, however harsh it might be toward Mr. Forrest, remembering the sarcasm in his voice the night before. But later, when Barb called them in for tea, still wiping at latent tears, she confided, "I hope this isn't getting you down. I do love him, you know. That's the trouble. I love him too much."

Maris was astonished. Her mother had never talked like this. Not only astonished, Maris was confused. It made her feel funny inside. Loving someone too much. That's what she had always imagined herself doing; she just hadn't imagined it would involve arguments and bad moods. She liked films where the man seemed remote and almost cruel, but softened in the end. She liked to imagine throwing her arms around a handsome man and have him reciprocate, squeezing the breath out of her with his embrace. Of course, that had never happened. She wasn't good at getting boyfriends. They always wanted to be simply that: a boy who was a friend.

Sophie had romances all the time. Maris's mother disapproved of them. When Sophie got dumped by John Hilliard, Maris's mother advised Sophie to forget him. Sophie said she would remember him always.

"What nonsense," Maris's mother said. "Now, Maris, I know you would never carry a torch."

Maris thought she would like to make up her own mind. She imagined it like the person who starts the Olympics, running with a great flaming torch, your heart bursting.

But it was hard to understand how Barb could fall in love with Derek Forrest if she knew he was so mean.

Maris tried to put herself into Barb's shoes and imagine she was married to him. Funny tingles went down her arms. She almost convinced herself she could suddenly feel his presence at that moment. There was something about the way he smelled. Not the aftershave, or something like perspiration. It was an elusive aroma, a taunting one, something odd and intangible. She smelled it now.

She jumped when she realized he actually was standing behind her.

"Sorry I startled you, Maris."

"It's okay." God, she thought, please don't let me go red again. She was so horrified at what she had been thinking. She was sure he knew.

His eyes, they could look at you in this piercing way and yet they could go blind, not looking at all, turning inward to some private dream.

"You're a very romantic girl, aren't you, Maris?" he asked.

Was he making fun of her?

"Why do you say that?" she asked, summoning anger, the only defense.

He shrugged. "Just an observation."

Well, keep it to yourself, she felt like saying. She hated him at that moment. It was as if he had put his fingers into her brain. He had no business there.

"I'll be out for a while," he said matter-of-factly now. "Barbara's upset. You'll see what you can do, won't you?"

She gaped at him. Did he actually expect her to be his ally? Why was he going out? Why was Barb so upset? "But Mrs. Forrest . . . she's really not well . . ."

He patted her shoulder. It was a gesture both intimate yet patronizing. "You'll manage. You're a clever girl."

Bastard, she heard herself thinking. She clamped her teeth onto her lips, afraid she might say it aloud. At that moment she thought she understood something about her mother.

CHAPTER NINE

At the time, she told herself she would never forget. But she did. Now she could only dredge it up as a memory of a memory. It was no longer sharp and clear. Some of it was wrong. Some of the details were mixed up with other people's stories, with other times, even with the things she saw in films.

The essence of it, though, remained etched in her mind, like fine lines on expensive glass, so that when she conjured up the memory, its essence tinkled softly, sharply, then disappeared, like chimes in the wind.

"Daddy," she had said. "Where are you going?"

"Never mind that," her mother had interrupted.

"I want to know."

"It's none of your business," the man said, but Maris

knew he was talking to her mother, not to her. For her he reserved a special smile. He looked down and gave it to her now. Then his expression shattered like smashed glass and it took Maris years to realize that the reason her father's smile had disappeared was because her mother had hit him, full in the face, and wiped the smile off and replaced it with anger and pain.

Ever after, his name was forbidden. If Maris mentioned Daddy, her mother said, "We don't need to talk about him, dear." Maris had tried to protest, but she was too young to know how to combat her mother's bitterness then, and when she was old enough to have made a better attempt, she had already been brainwashed about it: Talking about Daddy was something you didn't do.

Of course, she also hated him for abandoning her, for not remembering her birthday or even sending a Christmas card. It was only by chance that she found the torn envelope and letter in the garbage can. She would never have known, except they were having trouble with the raccoons who kept opening the lids at night and distributing the garbage all over the driveway. One morning it was early and cold, frost was like a layer of ash on the lawn, and her mother had looked out and seen all the trash, all their private garbage, strewn for the whole neighborhood to see: empty bottles of hair dye, chocolate wrappers, a wine bottle, worst of all the two scotch bottles that had been wrapped separately in a paper bag and tied up so the garbage man wouldn't see, and now were lying there exposed, the frost giving the bottles a glistening look. "Oh, my God," her mother had said.

"I'll go, I'm dressed, don't worry," Maris assured her, hurrying outside to pick it all up, forgetting her gloves and having to blow on her red hands as she retrieved their private business, a Tampax tube, a Sara Lee cake box, and the letter. Why she had even bothered to notice it especially, she would never know. Maybe it was inevitable, like a signal, her father calling out for her. She gave a quick glance up at the window to see if her mother was watching, and then she stuck the pieces, the ones she could find, into the pocket of her down jacket. She had recognized the handwriting. After all these years, she had recognized his beautiful handwriting, the curved perfect letters, the round dots above the *i*'s. The scraps stayed there, in her pocket, almost all morning at school, burning a hole in her brain, until she had a private moment after class to lay them out and piece them together. Some of it was missing.

> . . . .r Maris
> be with yo   th Christm but your mother tells
> on a trip going your school al   hope   ceive I
> sent
> . . . ways, Da

What trip, what Christmas, what plans, what sent? Her mind was reeling as she tore the bits into even smaller pieces and flushed them away down the girls' room toilet so that she wouldn't be tempted to take them and shove them into her mother's face.

She was afraid of a confrontation. To accuse her mother and present concrete evidence meant that everything would be changed forever. It was easier to live in the familiar than risk the unknown.

"Men, men, men," her mother said.

Maris dreamed of a knight coming down a long dirt road, riding a big horse that wore a cloak and blinders, that snorted in the cold, and the knight reached down and scooped her up and they rode off into a landscape she recognized well, with mountains and a lake in the distance and happily ever after amen.

But even though she had flushed the evidence away, she began making inroads. She'd ask casual questions and get evasive answers. Finally she risked it. It was Christmas and her mother was being particularly, unusually, nice. She had bought Maris the leather jacket she had wanted, even though it wasn't on sale before the holidays were over, even though the more usual thing would have been for her mother to tell her to wait, they'd get a jacket in January or even March, when nobody wanted them anymore, when the selections were picked over and perhaps her mother would forget all about it. But this Christmas she had taken

Maris with her to the mall and they chose the jacket and her mother paid with her credit card and it was the name on the card that jolted Maris, still her father's name: Andrew Pelham.

"Why doesn't he ever send me a present?" she blurted out.

Her mother's cheeks grew pink and she gave Maris a glance and the clerk a nod. "This is not the time or place for such a conversation, Maris."

"Why not?" Maris persevered.

Her mother just gave her a hateful look and dragged her from the store, but not without the big bag with the leather jacket inside. Maris felt ashamed. Her mother had finally bought her what she really wanted for Christmas and she had ruined it.

For a change, her mother didn't yell. Instead they went upstairs to the food hall and ordered coffee.

"He was impossible to live with," her mother said, leaning toward Maris confidentially.

"But that's between you and him," Maris said, surprising herself. "What does it have to do with me?"

Her mother sighed. "You don't understand. I can't live with a person like that for your sake. I have to think of my own life.

"He sends money for you every month," she added.

Maris wanted to accuse her mother, tell her about the letter, but her courage failed her.

"Don't look so miserable," her mother had said.

"Put yourself in my place. Think of living with some-one who acts sane one day and crazy the next. Who buys you a present, then snatches it away. A kiss one minute, a smack the next."

"He beat you?"

Her mother looked resigned. "No, not that way. Worse. I felt I was walking on eggs every minute." She pointed to her head. "Mental. Up, down, up, down, you never knew which way the wind was blowing." Her mother sipped coffee and reflected.

Maris felt warm inside. She had a vision of sharing more confidences with her mother, having long talks, becoming friends.

"He was crazy," her mother said abruptly. "Crazy people are unreliable. Remember that, Maris." The frown was back between her eyes. "Well, move your butt, maybe we can beat the traffic home."

The moment was lost.

Maris never told her about finding the letter. She lay in bed and imagined her mother walking on eggs, tak-ing itsy-bitsy steps, trying to hold her weight back from the fragile shells.

It was no way to live. Not being sure. Barb couldn't be sure of her husband. He was nice, then he wasn't. His eyes were alive, then dead. You never knew when the eggshells would break.

CHAPTER TEN

If it hadn't been for the children getting so upset, for refusing to cooperate, for making Maris look as if she weren't doing her job. If it hadn't been for a lot of things. Like Barb.

Instead of just staying in her room and keeping the argument private, she had to come downstairs in her robe, looking miserable and sick, and scream at Mr. Forrest in the hall.

"Please!" she cried. "Please!"

At first Maris was frightened. It was like the good Barb had been replaced with a bad Barb, a stranger. Maris wanted the other Barb back. She wanted the feeling of calm back. She wanted them to all feel like a family again. Then she felt sad. It had all been going so well.

"Please, Derek!" Barb cried.

Embarrassed, Maris closed the sitting room door. She and the children had been watching a nature program on television. Adam had explained they were only allowed to watch educational programs. Vicky nodded, making a face.

The subject was ants. The kids were fascinated by the ants cooperating with each other, building things and tearing them down. Maris told them about the time she put a big blade of grass across the entrance to an ant nest and how the ants had hurried out and one ant, bigger than the others, had seemed in charge. The ants moved the blade of grass away in no time at all.

"Then what?" Vicky asked. "Did you do it again?"

"That would have been mean."

"Ssssh," Adam said. "They're talking about ants in America. Do you know those ants, Maris?"

Maris had laughed and felt happy. The windows were open and the night air was soft and sweet. Then Barb had come down the stairs and started screaming. Mr. Forrest said nothing for a long time and then he let out a sound like a growl. It startled Maris and the children, and it made Barb stop. "That's enough!" he said.

That's when Maris shut the door. She turned up the volume on the TV, but the children only half watched and listened to the rest of the program. The other part listened to what was going on outside in the hall.

It was a relief when the front door slammed. There was no more screaming. The TV announcer blared. Music swelled with an advertisement for cars.

And then came the awful weeping. Agonized, strangled, like something from another world.

Oh, my God, Maris thought. What am I supposed to do now?

She stopped feeling frightened and sad. She felt betrayed. She wanted to scream at Barb and tell her to shut up, to tell her she had ruined everything and why, just for once, didn't things work out?

The children stopped paying attention to the TV altogether. Vicky's nose was red on the end and Adam looked stricken.

"Come on, guys," Maris said, trying to summon up strength to comfort them. "All parents have fights once in a while. It doesn't mean they don't love you." Vicky looked doubtful and Adam looked bored. Even to Maris's ears, the words sounded hollow.

Adam wrapped his arms around himself and refused to budge when the program was finally over and Maris said it was time to get ready for bed.

Vicky copied him.

"This is silly," Maris said.

A film began on the television, an old American film in black and white. Maris recognized John Wayne.

"We want to watch this," Adam said.

"It's American," Vicky added, as if to make it more permissible.

"It's cowboys," Adam said. "You can tell us about them like you did the ants."

"I don't know any cowboys," Maris said firmly. "It's time for bed."

"Bugger," Vicky said, and even Adam was shocked. But he wasn't going to cooperate, either.

"I'll have to tell your mother," Maris said, but this met only stony silence and eyes glued to the movie.

"You wouldn't want to upset her, would you? Not when she's already so upset."

"She's not upset with us," Adam said.

"She will be if you won't go to bed."

"It's summer. Who cares?"

"Yeah, who cares?" Vicky echoed.

Yeah who cares? Maris thought. Why should *she*? The place was a crazy house anyway. The father running out on the mother, the mother into throwing up — maybe she was anorexic, Maris thought suddenly — the kids cursing and swearing.

"Okay," Maris said. "But let's see what else is on. I don't want to watch this stupid movie."

That took some of the wind out of their sails, Maris thought. They looked surprised, but Adam got her the television section from the newspaper and they discussed what was better, the stupid cowboy movie or a comedy about a large family who lived in the north of England.

The children voted for the comedy, obviously something they had heard about but didn't normally get to stay up to see. Maris couldn't understand a word the people were saying. She was sorry she hadn't insisted on watching the cowboy film.

The children were just about falling off their feet by the time they had finishing watching the comedy, a detective show, and the late news, but they still refused to go to bed. Maris had lost some of her cool by then. She worried that Mr. Forrest would come in and find the kids still up. What if they fired her, asked her to go home? It would be awkward on this end and worse on the other. On the other end would be her mother's *I told you so* to listen to. She'd rather stick it out here, in spite of the atmosphere. Anyway, tomorrow Mr. Forrest would go off early and stay at work until late evening.

"That's it!" Maris said. "Up to bed, the two of you!"

The sun will come out tomorrow, she told herself, like the song. Everything will be better in the morning. She ushered the kids upstairs and didn't insist on them doing anything except getting into bed. But suddenly they were docile and obedient, brushing their teeth, washing hands and face.

They fell asleep almost immediately. Down the hall, Barb's bedroom door was closed. There was no way of knowing whether she was awake or not. Maris would have liked some guidance, some word from her. It scared her to have Barb like this. Maris felt alone and completely responsible. It was as if she were babysitting Barb, too.

She went back downstairs and straightened up the living room. She turned on the porch light and turned the lights off in the hall and kitchen. Then she was caught in a moment of terror when she heard something outside. A scratching, scrabbling sound. An animal.

The front door had no lock. This had disturbed her when she arrived, but she went along with Barb's casual attitude that nothing ever happened in this remote place. Maris had forgotten to worry about it. But that was when Barb and her husband had seemed like adults, people who could take care of things. Now she felt vulnerable. What if something tried to get in?

Maris forced herself to go to the window to look out. Knowing was better than imagining.

There was an animal out there. It moved stealthily through the garden. A fox? Mr. Forrest had talked about foxes. Nothing to worry about from a fox. But this thing looked too big. A dog, perhaps? Nothing to worry about from a dog, either.

But there was something strange in the way it was moving. It wasn't sniffing around the ground or getting into the garbage cans. It was pacing. Back and forth, back and forth. And its head was raised as if looking up at the bedroom windows. Maris's blood ran cold.

Visions of open windows, easily climbed into, unlocked kitchen and larder doors, unlatched everything swarmed in her mind.

She stepped back, suddenly aware that she might be seen. But this is stupid, stupid, stupid, she told herself. A dog isn't going to open doors or climb in windows.

She steeled herself and looked again. It was sitting in the middle of the garden, its head lowered now, its eyes seemingly full of light. Of course it was only her fear, imagination, she reminded herself. The creature wasn't really looking at her. Not the way she thought, straight at her. But she couldn't take her own eyes away. She felt instead drawn toward it, her whole body straining, as if she might crash through the glass of the window and be dragged across the lawn into its jaws.

She wanted to scream for Barb, but her mouth was dry; nothing came out. She clutched at the curtain so hard that it began to pull off its rod.

Her eyes burned. As if light and heat were radiating toward her, from its eyes, from its heart. Mixed up with her fear was a terrible sadness. She wanted to weep, from fear and grief. The beast showed its fangs, its teeth, and then, unbelievably, it smiled.

Maris forced her eyes closed. Her heart was in her ears and she felt as if she would faint. It was only her determination not to fail, not to let her mother win, that made her take a breath and look again.

The garden was empty. Nothing at all was there. She was aware of the sweat that drenched her body, the smell of fear from under her arms.

She crawled up the stairs to Barb's bedroom door. It didn't matter if Barb was sick or what, she needed to talk to someone, to get her sanity back. Without knocking, she turned the knob and opened the door. The room was pitch-black.

"Barb!" she called, finding her voice.

For a moment there was no answer, and then she heard the rustling of bedcovers and Barb's voice, sharp and hoarse, as if she had been lying there awake. "What's the matter?"

"I'm sorry to bother you. But there was a big dog in the garden. It was weird."

"A weird dog?" Barb's voice had an edge, as if it were trying to control itself on the edge of an abyss.

Even to Maris's ears it sounded ridiculous. A weird dog in the garden. Right.

"Is everything okay now?" Barb asked after a silence.

"I guess so. It's gone."

"That's all right, then."

"But Barb . . . it was so strange. It scared me."

"For heaven's sake. Go to sleep, Maris."

That was it. Dismissed. Barb hadn't even bothered to turn on the light. Maris felt defeated, dead tired. She went to her room and crawled into bed with her clothes on. She scrunched herself up into a ball and slowly tried to make herself believe it had been a hallucination. All the fighting, the screaming, had made her crazy. She was shivering.

She fell into a kind of wakeful sleep, her body starting every now and then as some frightening image appeared in her mind. She heard a car coming up the lane. Mr. Forrest coming home.

She listened to the slam of the car door, the crunch of footsteps on the path, the front door opening. She got up and crept across the floor to put her ear to the door. He had gone into the kitchen and was running water. Every sound became magnified: the switch on the electric kettle, the hiss as the water came to a boil.

Footsteps went from kitchen to sitting room. He was going in there to sit down and drink his coffee. Was he feeling sorry? Did he even care to know if she and the children were safe? She was no longer shivering with fear but trembling with rage that he had walked out and left her to cope with Barb and the children. She wanted to rush downstairs and berate him.

He was coming upstairs. Her bedroom door didn't have a lock, either. What was the matter with these people, with no locks on their doors? How did she even know it was him? Anyone could have come into the house. Anyone could walk in on her.

The footsteps stopped near her door. But it wasn't

her door that opened. He was looking in on the children. Suddenly worried about his kids. Obviously they were sound asleep. She heard their door being closed gently. She stopped breathing for a split second, until the footsteps retreated to the other end of the hall. She felt relief and anger. He had not even bothered to see if she was all right. He was supposed to be in charge. He was supposed to be the father.

She waited for what seemed a long time. Then she opened her door, willing it not to squeak, and stepped out into the hall.

She had no plan. She just felt anxious to see that the kitchen was normal, that a used coffee cup was in the sink, the kettle still a little warm, the dish towels hung neatly. She needed to see it was like that, to be sure there was no vomit, no blood, nothing out of the ordinary.

That's what she had been missing, she realized. The ordinary. Because aside from the fact that she was in a foreign country with different customs and habits, with speech that was the same but not the same — in spite of that, nothing here was ordinary. Not the woods, not the way Mr. Forrest's eyes changed from bright to opaque, not Agnes's bad moods or Barb's hysteria. Certainly not the rabbit hutch that must always be kept locked. A locked rabbit hutch when every other door was left open.

She tiptoed into the kitchen. The moon cast a long

blade of light across the tiled floor, slicing the room in two. She reached out to touch the kettle. It was warm. On the drainboard, a china cup was turned upside down, rinsed and waiting to dry. The towels hung neatly, stained only by shadows, not blood. But there was that smell in the room, the faintest hint of it, an odor she still had not been able to identify. It reminded her of something . . . but whatever it was scuttled back into a corner of her mind and refused to come out. What did I expect? she asked herself, feeling abashed. Am I looking for monsters like a child who checks under the bed before going to sleep? Even the ordinary can seem extraordinary when you're in a nervous state.

"Is there something wrong, Maris?" She jumped at the sound of the voice. Mr. Forrest's voice, but somehow hoarser than usual. He was close enough for her to have noticed if he had spent the evening drinking. She smelled nothing like that. He smelled instead of sweat. Clean sweat, the kind that comes from hard physical exercise. What had he been doing tonight?

"Did I wake you?"

"I wasn't asleep," Maris said coldly. She stepped back from him.

"Everything okay? Any problems?"

The words came out in a deluge. "The kids wouldn't go to sleep and there was a dog in the garden and I was scared to death. It isn't fair."

"Wait, slow down. The children are asleep now and they look fine. I'm sure you did a good job with them. What's this about a dog?"

"Never mind," Maris said. She stepped back again because he had come closer, as if to comfort her.

"It must have given you quite a fright."

"It did!" She glared at him.

"I'm sure it was only a fox. I told you about the foxes. They get in the trash bin."

"It wasn't a fox."

"Well, a dog, then; it's the same thing. Just out scavenging."

"There are no locks. Anything could happen here in the middle of the woods."

"Nothing will happen, believe me."

"How do you know?"

"I'll take care of it."

"Of what? Suppose it was some wild animal. Do you have a gun? And what difference does it make? You weren't here anyway."

He seemed to withdraw suddenly. He was still standing in front of her, but it was as if she had scalded him or chilled him to the bone.

"Guns are filthy objects," he said with contempt. "I should hate to live in your country. Isn't it true that everyone carries a gun?"

Maris had to laugh. "Not everyone."

"Let's not discuss guns."

There was a long silence in which Maris was aware that he was simply staring at her. The fear crept over her again. Why had he come down again? Didn't Barb care if her husband was in the kitchen talking to the au pair in the middle of the night? Once again, Maris felt unprotected by these people. What was expected of her now?

"You don't need to be afraid of me," he said very gently. Then he was gone, slipping out of the room as soundlessly as he had come in. The moonlight sliced the floor again. The towels hung in soldierly rows. Stained only by shadows, she thought. She stood for a long time, afraid that if she walked into the rooms of the dark house, something would be lurking, waiting to grab her.

"Don't be afraid," he had said. But the words were more disturbing than comforting. Was there something to be afraid of?

CHAPTER ELEVEN

The arrival of Agnes, moods and all, was just what was needed to switch things back to normal. Maris wasn't surprised that she had overslept and had missed the sound of Mr. Forrest's early morning departure. She had been up until all hours, unable to fall asleep. The unlocked bedroom door had bothered her, conjured up bad visions that seemed very real and possible in the middle of the night. The moon went down, or clouds obscured it, and her bedroom had been thrown into blackness. Staring at the door, to make sure it wouldn't open, had the opposite effect. The darkness bloomed into hideous blobs before her eyes, turned green and gold, made her feel blind, and made her see the door moving when it really wasn't. She had to resort to looking at the door sideways, keeping an eye on it out of the corner of her vision, so that it wouldn't slip and slide into its tricks.

Now the room was the way it was supposed to be. The door was closed, had never opened. It was another beautiful day. The children were already playing in the garden and Agnes was hanging the wash on the clothesline.

Maris put on a pair of shorts. She was anxious to get outside into the sun, to dispel all the memories of the night before. But she went down to the kitchen cautiously, uncertain about facing Barb. To her relief, Barb looked normal. Still pale, thin, and tired, but totally normal as she rolled her shampooed hair up on heated rollers. The sound of birdsong came in through the open window. Adam and Vicky laughed and even Agnes's drones sounded melodious. It's because *he*'s not here, Maris thought.

"I'm sorry about last night," Barb said.

"Me, too. I mean I'm sorry I acted like such a wimp, bothering you about the dog."

"Never mind," Barb said. "Make us some tea."

Maris was happy to have something to do. She was setting out cups and saucers when Barb said, "We've been unfair."

"What?"

"You'll go bonkers cooped up with us every day. I never gave it a thought until this morning."

"I don't understand. I came here to help."

"You have helped. And you can help some more. But you need a change once in a while. Some friends are coming over this afternoon. Two old dears. One of them is bringing her granddaughter."

It was the last thing Maris expected. Fixing her up with a friend. Fixed-up friends were always losers. It would be awful.

"She's your age," Barb went on, "and she lives in Kelton." When Maris looked blank, Barb added, "Kelton is a real town, with shops and a cinema. There's a bus, so you could visit each other. You like going to the movies, don't you?"

Maris knew she should show a little enthusiasm. She tried to summon some up. How bad could the granddaughter be? Maris could meet her on weekends and get away from the house when Mr. Forrest was home.

"There, you're smiling! You like the idea!" Barb said in a hopeful voice.

There's an air of an invalid about her, Maris thought. She's become sicker or something. She sounds different, as if she's grown years older in less than a week.

After her hair was dry, Barb wanted to bake a cake for tea, to serve to the old dears and the granddaughter. Maris offered to help.

Friends, she thought, as she stood at the kitchen window, washing up the breakfast dishes. Barb was concerned with getting Maris a friend, but what about Adam and Vicky? What had Adam said? Could he really have only one friend? It must be a lot different from America. But Adam and Vicky didn't seem to mind having only each other.

Maris greased the cake pans and broke the eggs into a bowl. Barb used an electric mixer, but even that tired her out. Maris took over, liking the way the batter became smooth as ecru silk.

"Cakes?" Agnes said as she pushed the mop around the floor, getting under their feet.

"We're having company," Barb said happily.

"Company." Agnes snorted. "You'll wear yourself out."

"It will do me good," Barb said, but it was a question, not a statement, as if she wanted Agnes to assure her.

"Making work for yourself," Agnes said, and picked up the bucket of soapy water. Maris could see how it strained the old woman's back.

"Let me help," she said.

She expected some retort, but Agnes gave what passed for a smile, a slight tightening of the lips. She let Maris take the handle. "Thanks very much, then."

Maris carried it outside to dump on the far end of the garden, where she had seen Agnes throwing water before.

Vicky came running up beside her. "Is it a jam tart?"

"It's a pail of dirty water."

"I mean what Mum's baking, silly. For the party."

"I'm not sure if it's called a jam tart," Maris said.

Vicky looked down her nose. "You never know anything, do you?"

Maris refused to be baited. "I've never seen a jam tart."

Vicky immediately looked abashed. "How sad for you."

Maris laughed. She put her hand under the bucket and held it over the grass at the end of the garden. Soapy water was good for killing aphids, Barb had said.

The water spilled in a long arch, suds holding back at the bottom of the bucket, too light to go first. In the sunlight the water became a rainbow. A dirty rainbow, tinged with red.

I'm not looking at that, Maris told herself, much in the way Vicky had once said not to look at only one magpie.

"Something wrong?" Barb said when Maris came back with the emptied bucket. "You've gone all pale."

Maris avoided Agnes's eye. "No, nothing. It's hot out there."

"It looks like we're in for a spell of beautiful weather," Barb said.

The cake had been put into the oven. The aroma of baking filled the kitchen. Nothing seemed safer than the smell of something baking.

* * *

The old ladies and the granddaughter arrived at three. One of the ladies drove the car, a big old-fashioned Rover. She sat very close to the steering wheel and squinted out the window, pulling the car up very close to the front door.

When they alighted, Maris agreed the thing to call them was old dears. They were jolly old ladies with pink cheeks and flower print dresses. They smiled and laughed and nodded their big noses toward Maris as they were introduced. Mrs. Dunkley and Miss Flood. Ethel and Gladys.

The granddaughter climbed out from the backseat, looking grumpy. Maris knew how she felt, being dragged around to meet someone who was supposed to turn into an instant friend. Her name was Brenda Finmore and she was a little shorter than Maris, but more broadly built, with muscular arms and cleavage sticking up over her T-shirt. Her face was made up, eyeshadow and blush and bright big rose-colored lips. She would have looked horribly cheap if it hadn't been for her hair, which was sleek chestnut and fell in perfect folds at the sides of her face. When she moved, the hair swung gracefully and fell right back into place. Hair to die for, Maris's friends would have said.

Brenda was Mrs. Dunkley's granddaughter. She wasn't Maris's age, she was nineteen. She didn't smile when she was introduced. Instead she lit a cigarette.

Maris felt intimidated by her voice. It was so self-assured and abrupt. She looked at Maris as if Maris were a specimen. She blew smoke through her nose.

"Cheers," she said.

Maris felt like a blob. Barb ushered them all inside, taking them through the house and back out into the garden. The old ladies chattered about the lovely weather.

"Brilliant," Ethel said.

"Lovely," Gladys agreed.

They sat down in the garden chairs and Maris went back in to get the tea tray. Barb had asked her to do this earlier and had apologized, saying she didn't want Maris to think she was being treated like a servant. It was just that Barb couldn't manage all the popping up and down and carrying things.

The tray held the cake that had been baked earlier and iced tea and coffee. The old ladies made admiring sounds and tucked in. From the conversation, Maris realized they had the idea Maris was Barb's younger sister. She wondered how well they knew Barb and where she had dug them up.

Mrs. Dunkley said she volunteered at a social services clinic. "I talk to people all over the U.K., and sometimes the States. Where do you come from, Maris?"

"Connecticut."

"Ah," Mrs. Dunkley said. "I have a friend in Colorado. Is that near you?"

"Oh, no, it's a thousand miles away."

For the first time, Brenda smiled. "America's a big place, Gran." She explained that you could put all of England into a couple of American states. There was no condescension in her voice. She sounded fond of her grandmother.

Maybe she's not so bad after all, Maris thought.

Adam and Vicky wore their best manners. Maris could see that Vicky was restraining herself from gobbling extra pieces of cake.

A little before five, Barb looked at her watch and became twitchy, as if anxious for the guests to leave.

Nothing had been arranged between Maris and Brenda. They had hardly spoken except for Maris to decline Brenda's offer of a cigarette every time she lit one of her own. Brenda smoked incessantly, smartly clicking her disposable lighter and crossing and uncrossing her legs. Maris couldn't imagine having anything in common with her and assumed the feeling was mutual. She didn't blame Brenda.

But before they all left, as they were all saying goodbye at the side of the car, Brenda said unexpectedly, "Like to come in to town on Friday?"

"Yes," Maris heard herself saying, equally unexpectedly.

"See you then. Cheers."

Brenda climbed into the backseat and the ladies got into the front.

"Musn't forget your recipes," Miss Flood said, and handed a manila envelope out the window to Barb.

"Thank you so much," Barb said.

"Do remember to tell us how they turn out," Miss Flood said.

"Oh, yes, I will," Barb said. Mrs. Dunkley put the car in gear and backed up slowly, her chin raised high as she checked in the mirror. She turned the car around and it went hesitantly down the lane. Brenda waved from the rear window, a cigarette between her fingers.

The moment the car was out of sight, Maris regretted having said yes to Brenda. Where was she supposed to meet her, and how? It was easier to just stick around here.

"Well, you two seemed to get along okay," Barb said as they went back into the house. Maris held her tongue in check. She was tempted to make a sarcastic remark about Brenda, but Barb looked so pleased, it would have been cruel. Avoiding further talk of Friday, Maris asked about the recipes.

Barb gave the manila envelope an offhand glance. "We belong to a cookery club. We try things out and report back."

Maybe part of Barb's problem was boredom. How

could she enjoy going to a cooking club with a bunch of old ladies? Maris tried to imagine Barb giving a report on a recipe. It was an incongruous picture.

Derek Forrest's car pulled into the driveway half an hour later. Maris sensed a change in the atmosphere that was becoming familiar. The warm summer afternoon became chilled with tension. Even when he scooped the kids up and laughed and cracked jokes, Maris felt wary. She couldn't be sure the sunny mood would stay. Crazy, she thought, remembering her mother walking on eggs. Crazy people are unreliable.

"And how's our Maris today?" he asked, turning his eyes on her.

"Fine," Maris said, and trembled. It was an intimate look. His voice, too, carried hints of collusion, as if they had shared some secret last night in the kitchen, as if something had happened between them. Maris was afraid to look at Barb.

She went into the kitchen. The afternoon tea things had already been washed. Barb had seemed intent on getting everything out of the way before Derek came home, almost as if she wanted to hide it from him. Maris didn't plan on blabbing anything, if that's what Barb wanted, but surely she didn't expect the kids to lie?

Maris called them in to set the table, and began peeling potatoes. Whatever Derek and Barb were doing, at least they weren't arguing. It was peaceful, with the sound of water boiling for the potatoes, the clink of dishes and cutlery being placed on the table.

And then Adam did something odd. He removed the leftover jam tart from the cake stand and stowed the slices in a biscuit tin. He carried the stand to the sink and began to wash it.

"You'll cut yourself!" Maris cried, afraid he would drop the heavy glass that was now slippery with sudsy water. She took it out of his small hands and rinsed it herself. "That was nice of you, Adam. But you didn't have to do that."

"Yes, I did," Adam said. Vicky quietly pushed the biscuit tin to the back of the kitchen dresser, and both of them went back to arranging the napkins at each place.

At dinner, the afternoon tea party was not mentioned. Crazy, Maris thought. What, was Derek going to be jealous that he had not been invited?

CHAPTER TWELVE

As the week neared its end, Maris wondered if she had been too quick to judge the Forrests. The week had passed peacefully, without arguments. Barb's health improved. She napped every afternoon while Maris watched the children. The days had passed in a haze of sunlight and flowers.

Brenda phoned late Thursday, just when Maris was sure she had forgotten. Brenda said leave it to her, she would plan everything, just meet her in Kelton. Barb got the bus schedule out.

"Where's she off to?" Mr. Forrest asked.

"To see the daughter of a college friend of my mother's. You know how she is. The minute she heard Maris was here, she wrote and arranged a get-together."

Maris held her tongue, but she wondered why Barb lied. Mr. Forrest offered to pick Maris up and bring her home. "Save her waiting for the bus at all hours," he said.

"Oh, no, she can catch the nine o'clock bus," Barb was quick to object. "It won't even be dark. After all, Maris is an adult, not a baby. She needs to get off on her own a bit."

Maris felt annoyed. They talked about her as if she weren't there. Nobody had bothered to ask her if she preferred the bus or a ride. Actually, though, she agreed with Barb, but not for the same reasons. Normally she would have liked a ride home, but not with Derek Forrest. They had managed to survive the week without a problem, she was feeling almost as if all her worries about him had only been imagination, but she still didn't like the idea of being alone in the car with him. Kelton was half an hour's drive — thirty minutes too long, as far as Maris was concerned.

Because Agnes prepared and left them a cold supper every Friday, Maris had the idea that Friday was the Forrests' regular night out. She had asked Barb if it was all right to meet Brenda on a Friday. Barb reassured her. "We don't go out often," she said. "We're homebodies, mostly."

Maris, remembering the previous Sunday, with Mr. Forrest disappearing on some private excursion, said nothing to contradict her. Barb was looking better but still too thin and pale. Her eyes were sunk into hollows. Maybe Mr. Forrest was one of those people who couldn't handle sickness. Her mother had a friend whose husband had walked out after a car accident left her paralyzed. The wife had been philosophical. He couldn't handle it, she said. She got married to someone else a year later.

In spite of Barb's words about treating Maris like an adult, she changed into a motherly nag just before Maris left. Did Maris have enough money, the right change for the bus, did she know how to use a public pay phone, and would she remember to buy postcards?

"You should have sent one to your mother by now."

Maris must have looked unenthusiastic because Barb persevered. "I know you haven't written to her. All she's had is that phone call to tell her you'd arrived. I'm sure she misses you."

But I don't miss her, Maris thought. If she was going to send any postcards to people she missed, it would be to Mrs. Li.

"I already bought some," Maris said. "Last week when I took the kids to Banfield."

"But you haven't sent them," Barb persisted.

Maris sighed. Amcrica suddenly seemed far, far away.

"I'll do it soon."

Barb drove her into Banfield to catch the afternoon bus to Kelton. The nine o'clock return bus, fortunately, would continue to the next village, past the Forrests' lane, so there would be no need to change.

"Take care," Barb said. "Say hello to Brenda for me." Maris felt like asking how long she had known Brenda and the two old dears, but the bus was snorting as if ready to depart. She climbed on and fumbled with the fare. She slipped into a rear seat and looked out the window. Barb was still standing there.

Why doesn't she go back home? Maris forced herself to smile and wave good-bye again. But Barb seemed determined to stay planted on the spot until the bus left.

At last the driver stopped talking to someone standing outside and closed the door. The bus moved away. Maris watched Barb watching her.

Maris concentrated on paying attention to the stops. The bus driver wasn't calling them out the way Barb said he would. She was supposed to get off at Precinct Centre. There would be a Lloyd's Chemist Shop on the corner, you couldn't miss it, Brenda had said, Kelton was a big town, you couldn't mistake any of the intermediate villages for it. Maris hoped so.

She need not have worried. She knew they were nearing Kelton when the hedgerows were gone and sidewalks appeared. The road widened, lined with gas stations and commercial buildings. The bus driver must have noticed her anxious stares in the mirror. As the bus swung into a crowded mix of shops, he called out, "Precinct Centre."

Maris got off the bus and looked around for the chemist shop. Brenda was slouching against the display window smoking a cigarette. She was wearing tight black jeans and a T-shirt that showed her bare midriff. When she saw Maris, she dropped the cigarette and stamped it out with her sandaled foot.

"You found it, then?"

"Sure. No trouble."

"Want to have a look around the shops?"

Maris did. It was tempting, all this merchandise; she felt as if she had been living a sheltered life for two weeks. She had promised Sophie a souvenir. She had brought fifteen pounds, nearly thirty dollars, to spend.

Brenda checked her watch. "We've got a while."

"Till what?" Maris asked, following Brenda toward the entrance to a shopping arcade.

"Go 'round the shops, then meet my mates for coffee."

"I didn't know we were meeting anyone."

"You'll get on with them. I said you were visiting from the States. Pat will ask you a lot of stupid questions about America. Don't take any notice."

They walked through some clothing stores and Maris was surprised at how expensive everything was. They looked around a bookstore, where Brenda leafed through fashion magazines. There were some mugs with pictures of the queen or Princess Di, the kind of thing Maris would have bought for souvenirs, but she felt embarrassed to buy them in front of Brenda.

They went to look at cosmetics. Brenda asked advice on nail polish and lipstick. She made a face at Maris's subdued choices. She went for blinding colors. Maris thought they were tacky but didn't say anything. She was suddenly aware of Brenda's scrutiny. "You've got nothing on, do you? We'll have to put that right before we go to the pub, later."

Maris glanced into the mirror on the counter. "What's wrong with how I look?"

"No makeup, you wally!" Brenda laughed. "You look about twelve."

Maris was flustered. "I don't think I have any lipstick with me," she stammered. She hardly ever wore makeup and hadn't had any on since she'd arrived.

"We'll soon fix that."

Brenda dragged her back out into the arcade and into a public ladies' room. She dumped her purse out onto the shelf under the mirror and fumbled through a heap of makeup to find what she wanted.

"Now, you just watch," she said, and Maris saw herself transformed from a pale, slightly freckled girl with unnoticeable brows and lashes into somebody around thirty. Makeup foundation turned her skin beige. Freckles diminished while eyebrows and eyelashes emerged, feathery brown arcs, lashes full and thick with bits of mascara beading moistly at the tips. Brenda brushed pink blush on her cheeks and lined her lips in red. She filled in the outline with pink lipstick and stood back to admire her handiwork. "There, what do you think?"

Maris thought she looked overdone, like a little kid playing dress-up, her lips pouty, her cheeks clownish. She rubbed some of the blush off, hoping Brenda would think she was just blending it better. There was a tell-tale line of beige against the whiter skin of her jaw. "It looks great," she said.

"You look brilliant!" Brenda proclaimed. "Come on, Pat and Kerry will be waiting."

She scooped up her belongings and threw them back into her purse. They went through the arcade to a busy coffee shop. Maris felt self-conscious in the makeup but, surprisingly, less nervous. This wasn't Maris Pelham going to meet Brenda's friends, it was some actress playing a part. The friends, she thought, would be like Brenda, girls who wore makeup and smoked and worked as clerks in offices — that's what Brenda said she did.

Maris followed Brenda to a table where two young men looked up and smiled. Brenda stopped to talk. Maris looked around, wondering which of the many girls sitting at tables with shopping bags of purchases at their feet they would be meeting.

"She's miles away," one of the boys said. Brenda

poked her arm. "Hey, sleeping beauty, we're talking to you. Meet Kerry and Pat."

Maris smiled the best she could. She hadn't expected boys. She wondered which guy was meant for her. Both of them were tall, with chiseled faces of an unfamiliar type. She couldn't size them up the way she could have with an American. They looked the picture of innocence one minute and devilish the next. One of them spoke in gulps, with an accent Maris couldn't understand. He was reading a newspaper that Maris recognized as the *Sun*.

Brenda had pulled out a chair and sat down. There was an empty chair between Kerry and Pat. Maris sat down, too. She glanced at the newspaper, for lack of anything else to do. Pat and Brenda were soon deep in conversation. That's it, Maris thought. This Kerry person is for me. The one with the gulps. He looked at her and she looked at him. He cleared his throat. She noticed his bobbing Adam's apple. He was nervous. Maybe he wouldn't be too bad.

He asked her a question and pointed at the newspaper. She figured out that he was indicating one of the articles. She looked down and read about another series of animal attacks, this time on sheep. Farmers demanded action. A crying shame that there were people who didn't care what their dogs got up to, the sheep farmers said. Load of rubbish, said the accused dog owners. Maris remembered the picture of Laddie.

She turned away, hoping not to see more photographs of murdered dogs.

"What'ch you make of it?" Kerry said.

"Who knows?" It was an inadequate answer, and silence fell between them. Maris felt ashamed. At least he had tried.

"Do you believe it's dogs?" she asked, giving him another chance.

"Nah." He folded the newspaper and tossed it aside. "Blaming dogs! Dogs don't do that."

"Attack sheep?"

"They'll do that all right, but not the way it says here." He tapped the newspaper. "A dog will worry a sheep, bite its leg, drive it to distraction, even over a cliff, maybe. But a dog would nae tear out a sheep's throat." He gave her a flinty smile. "Anyway, I've heard a gorier theory."

He didn't elaborate. Maris wanted to keep the conversation going, at least as much of it as she could understand. "Like what?"

"Och, maybe wilder creatures. Something unhuman?"

Maris waited to hear more, but he stopped again. "Would ye like some coffee? Pat, get us two coffees, would you?"

"Get them yourself."

"Get me one, too, then," Brenda demanded. Pat and Kerry got up to go to the counter. Brenda turned to

Maris with an expression like a clucking mother hen. "Well, you two seem to be getting on. Like him?"

"He's fine. But I wish you had told me you were going to fix me up."

"It's nothing serious!" Brenda screeched. "Don't worry, he won't expect anything. If he tries it on, tell him your age. He'll go berserk." She roared with laughter.

"Doesn't he know how old I am?"

"Are you crazy?"

They were coming back. "And don't you say anything," Brenda warned.

Maris wondered if Kerry was the type to try it on, as Brenda put it. He seemed awkward and gangly and maybe a little stupid, speaking in that dopey accent. Like a thick farm boy in a film. He slopped some of the coffee into the saucer as he put the cup down.

"It's cappucino," he said earnestly. "I hope you like it."

"Thanks," Maris said, and decided she meant it. Her former apprehension was replaced with a kind of giddy recklessness. It was going to be a nice evening. She wasn't going to worry about a thing.

CHAPTER THIRTEEN

You only had to be eighteen to be admitted to a pub, but nobody paid any attention to Maris. She had been carefully rehearsing her birthdate, changing the year so she'd be older. No one asked for her ID. She and Brenda sat down at a small round table while Kerry and Pat went to get the drinks. The three of them wanted pints of beer. Maris didn't want to drink alcohol, but she didn't know what to order instead. Brenda gave her a sharp glance when Pat asked "What'll you have?" and Maris, flustered, said she didn't know the brands here. They had already been incredulous about her not smoking. She felt, in Brenda's own words, like a wally — a stupid fish out of water. Brenda suggested a shandy. "She's not used to British beer," she said to the boys.

A shandy turned out to be a mixture of beer and fizzy lemonade. Maris was silently grateful to Brenda for the suggestion.

The jukebox played and people talked and laughed and, over it or under it, Maris could hardly understand a word Kerry said. She smiled at what she hoped were appropriate places in his conversation. She nodded her head when he seemed to be indicating a need for affirmation. What he was talking about, she realized suddenly when the music momentarily died down, was the article in the *Sun*, the mauled sheep.

"Something unhuman, what I said."

"Sorry? I didn't catch all that."

"Are ye interested in that kind of stuff?"

"I don't know that much about it."

Kerry leaned toward her and lowered both chin and voice. He cast a suspicious glance at Pat and Brenda, indicating that what he was about to say was private.

"What I heard is . . ." he said. He paused for effect.

"Yes?"

"Is that it's Martians."

"Oh, for . . ." Maris turned away angrily.

"What's he been telling you, love?" Pat asked in a way Maris felt was overly familiar.

"Load of rubbish," she retorted, remembering the news article. To her surprise, it made a hit. They all laughed, good-naturedly this time. Kerry had the grace to look slightly abashed.

While they were ordering what was on the menu — chicken pot pies with chips and peas — Pat offered to buy the next round of drinks. Brenda explained that it was the protocol. "We'll buy the next round," she told Maris.

"More of the same?" Pat asked.

"I'll have just a plain lemonade this time, please," Maris said. The shandy had gone to her head a little, mixed with the noise and smoke of the pub; it seemed as if everyone in England smoked like a chimney.

With the unintelligible Kerry at her side, she was acutely aware that she was in another country. Exotic, in a way, even if it was only a pub, and more like an American hangout at that, with a jukebox and video games in the corner. Had she been saying she missed the ordinary? The strangeness of the voices, the smells, were more intoxicating than beer.

Pat brought back the drinks. A waitress followed with their dinners. Maris marveled at the huge mound of peas on each plate. Before they had finished, Brenda was getting up to buy another round. "Lemonade?" she asked Maris. Maris nodded. Brenda and Pat exchanged glances and laughed. Maris knew they were poking fun at her drinking lemonade, but she ignored it. She was suddenly feeling very content and happy. Everything had taken on a rosy glow, even her mother.

Now she could look at her mother objectively, from so far away, and see what a pathetic person she was.

"Pathetic old cow," Brenda was saying about an older woman at the bar.

"Yes . . ." Maris said, "that's just what I was thinking." Brenda's face seemed to move out of range and Maris had to lean forward to get her back in focus. "I was just saying to myself that my mother is a pathetic old cow." She took another swig of lemonade to wash down the taste of the greasy chips. "But I understand her now. I just realized that." She looked around the table, but nobody seemed to think it was a marvelous revelation. Pat and Brenda were laughing again. Maris laughed, too, pretending she had meant it as a joke. They didn't want to hear about her problems in a place like this. Not when they were having such a good time. Maris felt nostalgic for a moment, and had a sudden longing to talk to Ms. Epstein, to tell her that they had misjudged her mother. She wondered if she could make a long-distance call on the pub's pay phone.

"What time is it in America?" she asked, breaking into the conversation going on around her.

"Why?" Brenda asked. "Have to phone mum?"

This sent them into gales of laughter. But Kerry stopped and frowned. He's a drag, Maris thought. Brenda didn't mean any harm. But the idea of phoning Ms. Epstein had reminded her of something else. Something she should do.

"It's your turn to buy a round," Brenda said.

Maris let go of the nagging thought. "Okay."

"You have enough money, don't you?" Brenda asked.

Kerry overheard. "Listen, I'll get it," he said, and moved his chair. Maris stopped him. She wanted to do the right thing, be part of it all. She groped in her pocket for a five-pound note and got up. Her leg knocked against the table, rattling the dirty plates and glasses.

"Let me," Pat said, and took the note from her hand.

Maris sat down. She felt unsteady.

"You all right?" Kerry asked.

"Of course."

But she glanced down at the greasy plates and felt sick. Kerry looked at her and got up from the table and went to the bar. He and Pat began to talk, then argue.

Maris wanted to ask Brenda what the problem was, but the words came out wrong.

Kerry came back. "Right," he said briskly. He put his hands under her arms and pulled her up. Maris realized she was drunk. She tried to ask for the ladies' room.

"Out you go," Kerry ordered, and marched her to the door.

"Ugh," she moaned. "I'm going to be sick."

"I know," Kerry said.

She started to push him off, but staggered and almost fell. She let him hold her arm after that. He took her outside to the pub garden, where people were sitting at tables and drinking under the trees. The pub had been so dark and now the light burned her eyes. Kerry pulled her to the side.

He didn't even try to turn his head to give her privacy.

"That's a waste of good money," he said crudely as her dinner came up.

Between retches, she tried to apologize. She felt appalled that a stranger would see her in such a state.

"Never mind, you didn't realize. They spiked your lemonades with vodka."

"What?"

"It was only meant as a joke. Nobody meant you to get sick."

Maris wiped her lips the best she could with a tissue. She felt only slightly better. Her mouth tasted terrible.

"I better go home," she said, looking around at the brightly lit garden. "Oh, my God."

"Going to be sick again?"

"I thought when we came out that it was daylight. It's already dark!"

Kerry looked around. "Yeah. It's dark."

"What time is it?"

Looking blank, Kerry took her hand and held it up so that she could read her own watch.

"Oh, my God."

"What's the matter?"

"I was supposed to be on the nine o'clock bus."

"So what's the big deal? Ten o'clock on a Friday night is hardly the end of the world."

"She'll say I always do this. She'll say it proves I'm unreliable. If Barb tells her, I'll have to go home."

"You need coffee first." Kerry took her elbow and steered her out of the pub garden. "Who's she and who's Barb?"

"Barb's who I work for. I take care of her kids. Didn't Brenda tell you?"

"She only told me that I had a date with a dishy American bird."

They were walking toward the same shopping mall she and Brenda had visited earlier. The shops were dark, but a pink neon glow came from the coffee bar.

"A little coffee will get you all sorted out."

"That's weird," Maris said. "Suddenly I can understand you perfectly."

"What? Oh, that was just part of the joke."

"What joke?"

"Brenda's idea. Lay it on thick for the tourist."

Maris pulled her arm out of his grasp.

"It was only a joke! No harm done."

"Making a fool out of someone isn't a very good joke."

"Look, I'm sorry," Kerry said, but he looked impassive.

They walked up the chrome stairs to the coffee bar. The pink lights and shadowy corners made the place more glamorous than it had been in daylight. Kerry brought her a cup of strong coffee. As she drank it down, she noticed a pay phone in the corner.

"It'll be all right," she said, as much to assure herself as Kerry. "I'll phone Barb and tell her I'll be late."

"Got enough change?"

She realized that Brenda had not given her the change from the five pounds for the round of drinks. She had some coins and the ten pounds she had planned to spend on souvenirs.

She glanced at her watch. This would be just about the time Barb would expect her. She dialed quickly. Barb answered immediately.

"Maris! Where are you? The bus went by fifteen minutes ago."

"I'm sorry. I lost track of the time. I didn't realize you could see the bus from the house."

"The children and I walked down to meet you. I let them stay up especially. They were so disappointed. Are you all right? Should we come to pick you up?"

Maris had a guilty vision of them standing at the end of the lane. She hadn't meant to disappoint them.

"I . . ." she stammered. How could she explain what had happened? A story of being tricked into getting drunk was the ultimate dumb excuse.

"Brenda and her friends are driving me home. That's

why I just didn't think about the time, not having to catch the bus. I'm really sorry, Barb."

"Okay. It's not the end of the world," Barb said, echoing Kerry. "But just how late do you plan to be?"

Barb didn't sound angry, but she didn't sound happy, either.

Holding her hand over the phone, Maris motioned to Kerry. "Do you have a car?"

Kerry shook his head.

"Is there a taxi?"

"You can call a minicab," he said doubtfully.

Maris signaled him to be quiet and told Barb she'd be back by eleven-thirty. Twelve at the latest.

"Midnight is *it*, Maris," Barb said sternly. "Earlier would be better." She hung up on Maris's apologies.

Maris slung the receiver into its cradle. "This was her idea, not mine! I didn't ask to meet Brenda. It's not my fault if Brenda's a bitch!"

"Steady," Kerry said. "Look, you don't have to defend yourself to me."

"I'm tired of being blamed for other people's mistakes."

"Missing the bus was your mistake."

Maris turned on him. "Really?"

"Well, you knew what time you had to go," Kerry said with maddening logic.

"I was supposed to remember when I was blind drunk?"

Kerry laughed uneasily. "Don't act like you never had a drink before."

"I never drink."

Too late, Maris realized it didn't sound convincing. Kerry wasn't buying it and neither would Barb.

He gave her a disgusted look. "Where did Brenda dig you up? I thought I was in for a bit of fun tonight."

Maris gaped. "What did you expect to happen?"

"Don't get your knickers in a twist. I just meant a meal, a drink, maybe a peck good night if I was a good boy. Look, there's a minicab phone over there."

Maris fingered the ten-pound note in her pocket. "How much do you think it will cost?"

"I haven't got a clue."

"Maybe I should check on another bus."

"I haven't got a clue about buses, either." He was impatient. "You do what you want, but make up your mind before Christmas."

Maris asked for a minicab to pick her up at the coffee bar. They said "Right," but when she told them she was going to Banfield, they hedged. It was late, not enough drivers, too long a trip.

Maris took a chance. "I'll give you ten pounds." She hoped it was more than the actual fare.

It worked. "Be right there, love," the man said.

Maris told Kerry not to bother waiting.

CHAPTER FOURTEEN

The minicab didn't show up for half an hour. Maris was about to phone again when she saw a car come into the precinct parking lane and flash its lights. Only some vague writing on the door indicated that it might be a cab. She walked over cautiously and peered in at the driver, who peered back at her from the open window.

"You ordered a taxi?" he asked in an accented voice.

Maris got into the backseat. She felt anxious, even though she made out KELTON CAR HIRE printed on the door. Only when the driver turned around to look at her, gave her a smile, and said "Banfield, right?" did she relax.

The roads were empty and the cab went a lot faster

than the bus and made no stops. She thought she might get back well before twelve if the driver kept the speed up. He didn't say much, just concentrated on driving, and she was thankful for that. She didn't feel like talking to anyone; she just wished she could crawl into bed. She had a splitting headache and her mouth tasted like a dirty sock. But first there would be Barb to face and, worse, Mr. Forrest.

Automatically, Maris began her defense. It didn't seem fair to be blamed for something she had no control over. She'd tell Barb the truth because Barb really should know about Brenda. Just because Brenda was some nice old lady's granddaughter didn't mean she was nice herself. Brenda and Pat and even Kerry, all of them had treated her like a joke. Like cats playing with a mouse. Maris stopped. The image had come too readily. She wasn't a mouse. She would never be a mouse ever again.

At last they came into Banfield. The shops were shut and dark; a single streetlight gave off a dim yellow glow at the end of the Parade. The taxi slowed. "What street exactly do you want?"

"Oh," Maris said, leaning forward. "Down the road that way. My house isn't right in Banfield."

"Not in Banfield?"

"Well, it's Banfield but a little ways out. I think they call it Banfield Vale."

The driver was shaking his head. "Is it not to Banfield you said you wanted to go?"

"I know I said Banfield. But I need to go a little farther down the road. To Wood End Lane."

"I am sorry, but that I cannot do," the driver said. He sounded truly regretful. "Banfield is what you said and Banfield is where I have taken you. Ten pounds, please."

Maris looked around. The village was deserted. She felt certain there would be no more buses tonight. "But I'm a visitor here," she pleaded. "I wasn't exactly sure. I mean, I said Banfield so you would know. Really, it's only down the road."

"I am truly sorry. But I will be off duty now. It is past the usual time."

"But how am I supposed to get there?"

He thawed a little. "Tell me, is there nobody at home?"

Was he trying to find out if she was going to an empty house? If she said nobody was home, would he agree to take her there and maybe attack her? "Of course there are people home. They're waiting for me. They'll be worried if I don't show up."

The driver pointed to a phone box. "Perhaps they will come to fetch you?"

She could see by his face that he wasn't going to budge. Maris felt in her pockets. All she had was a bunch of coins — not enough for a bribe. Why hadn't Brenda given her the change?

She gave it one more try. "What's the usual fare from Kelton to Banfield?"

The driver was wily. "Ten pounds. Plus tip."

Maris opened the door and got out of the taxi. "I only have enough to make a phone call," she said adamantly. She strode purposefully to the phone booth and picked up the receiver. She had no intention of calling Barb. There was still time, if she jogged, to get to the house around midnight. She'd take the footpath. She pretended to dial and then talk, watching the taxi out of the corner of her eye. He was still there, the rat. *I am going off duty now.* What happened to that?

"You don't have to wait around," she called to him nastily.

"Will they be coming for you, then?"

"None of our business."

He shrugged. Maris waited until the taxi was out of sight. Then she set off. The streetlight leaked its yellowish glow as far as the stile. She climbed over onto the footpath. As she walked away from Banfield, the light dimmed. Suddenly it was extinguished, like a match, gone. She was plunged into darkness. It had never occurred to her there would be no lights along the road. A few nights ago the moon had been high and bright, but now, as she searched the sky, there was only the faintest glow from a waning disk covered by cloud. My eyes will get used to it, she thought. In the meantime, she could follow the fence easily, just keep her hand on it lightly, and walk straight beside it.

After a while, her eyes did adjust and she could walk faster. Above the field, the treeline was a continuous black hulking shape. But there was no need to get scared. The worst thing was that she couldn't read her watch to check on the time. Once in a while, she risked running.

Maybe it was because of the rhythmic sound of her own breathing and the beating of her shoes on the path that she hadn't heard the other sound. It was only when she stopped to catch her breath that she was aware of something else stopping a fraction of a second later, an accompanying rhythm, accompanying breathing.

No, that was imagination. She was letting her imagination run away with her. She was determined to get herself back to the Forrests' cottage, probably get chewed out, tell Barb the truth about what happened. The truth was the best defense, Maris realized as she set off again, heartened by the slight brightening of the gibbous moon as the cloud cover moved across the sky with the wind. It was such a simple thing, stupid not to have realized it before. The truth would have been the easiest excuse all these years.

"Tell them you're not feeling well, Maris," her mother would say, whenever there was a conflict, one party better than another, or something too boring to go to. "Tell them you've got an upset stomach and can't come."

"I don't really want to go anyway."

"People don't want to hear things like that! But they're sympathetic if you say you're ill."

A million good excuses to make Barb sympathetic crammed into Maris's head. But she'd tell the truth. The taxi driver had refused to take her farther than Banfield. She only had ten pounds. She had never expected to be ditched by Brenda and her friends. She thought Barb —

The sound was there. Unmistakably the sound of breath. Panting breath, much louder and more powerful than Maris's breathing. And movement. Moving up there in the woods, keeping pace with her, following her, watching her, stopping and starting with her.

A fox? A dog? Another dog like the one in the garden, with glittering eyes and a wicked smile? Dogs could bite, could push you over a cliff. But a dog was man's best friend. A dog understood commands. A dog could be cowed by harsh words.

"I'm not afraid of you," Maris called out. Her voice was less convincing than she'd planned. She cleared her throat and began again. "I'm not — "

There was a sudden snarl, quick and fierce. It hung palpably in the air, as if it had a shape and odor all its own. The looming trees were threatening now, smug as ogres with the possibilities of things lurking behind them. Even the surface of the field grew alive with twisting shadows that could easily be snakes or the low crouches of long-tailed slithering beasts. A hollow hooting came through the darkness like an omen.

"Go, go," it said in warning. Just an owl. The wind picked up and put a thousand whispers into her ears, tickling and teasing her. Something in her chest was heavy, leaden, making her slow to a stop. She wanted to run, but her legs were like logs. She sensed something coming out of the trees, making its way toward her; as slow as dream syrup, it was moving on four legs.

Please please help please, this is stupid, Maris don't be afraid I am but don't run run I'll be good, I promise, I promise, don't please hurt me no.

She realized she was speaking aloud, the words a prayer of nonsense thoughts and wishes, dreams. Safety loomed in her mind like something she would never have again.

Her voice frightened her as much as the thing up there near the trees. She could tell its shape because it was a paler dark than the surrounding dark, if that made any sense.

Oh, it's just a dog. No, something wrong with the way its legs moved in a furtive feral gait.

"Go away!" She tried to scream the words, but they stuck in her mouth like heavy gluey lumps. Out of her open mouth came only terrified silence that ached in her jaws and squeezed at her throat. "Go . . . awaaaaay!" She sounded like an animal herself. "Oh, please leave me alone," she cried, knowing she was unable to do anything more than wait for it to reach her.

The woods seemed to go uncannily quiet. Maris could feel, even though she couldn't see its eyes, that the animal was considering her, appraising her, setting its sights. She held her breath until it gave way in small muted gasps, like whimpers. Then there was a soft sound of a matching whimper from the animal. Hope against hope, it seemed to be retreating back into the trees. One final yelp stopped cold, as if choked off. And then the normal sounds of night resumed, comforting in a mysteriousness that was merely ordinary.

A cold sweat of relief drenched her face and hair, made her clothes cling clammily. Perhaps it had been only a dog after all, trying to find its way home. Poor dog. Poor Maris.

She took a tentative step forward. Another. Then she ran. She noticed ahead the faintest glimmer of light. It seemed to take forever to get near enough to see what it was: the porch light of Milestones, the house at the turning to the lane to the Forrests' house.

With relief came elation and the crazy idea that she could sneak into the house and up to bed. It was shattered by the vision of Barb's distraught form straining from the lit doorway.

"Maris! For God's sake. What happened to you?"

"I'm okay, I'm okay. I'm sorry you were worried. I can explain."

Barb looked at her incredulously, then looked past her, searching the dark lane with wild, worried eyes. "Did you see him?"

Maris shivered with renewed fear. "Who?"

"Derek. He went out to find you. How can you not have seen him? He drove to Banfield to pick you up; we knew you would be stuck there. I waited for your call."

Maris was bewildered. She wanted to get inside, to sit down, to explain, to go to the bathroom, but Barb was rooted in the doorway. Finally, Maris just pushed past and, zombielike, Barb followed. Like the slicing of a knife, her words cut into Maris's back.

"Is this the thanks I get for trusting you?"

"It wasn't my fault. I really tried to get home by twelve but — "

"Don't make excuses. You lied. Brenda phoned. She was concerned because you insisted on taking a taxi. She had no idea why you ran off. We had to call the taxi company and they told us the driver was taking you to Banfield."

"I didn't have enough money."

Barb shook her head and beads of perspiration hit Maris's cheeks. She could suddenly smell Barb's sweat, the acrid smell of fear. Barb grabbed her by the shoulders.

"Where in heaven's name is Derek?"

"I don't know. I didn't see him."

Barb's fingernails were cutting into her bare arms. "That's impossible. There's no other road. You must have seen his car."

"I didn't, Barb, honest. I would have been glad to see a car. I would have flagged it down. Something was following me out there, some animal . . . I . . ."

"What are you saying?" Barb's skin, red with the flush of anger, went white as the moon.

"An animal in the woods. But I'm okay, really. Whatever it was stopped following me." Barb, get a grip, Maris thought. I'm the one that thing was after. "Look, what's the big deal? I'm here and I'm safe. I'm sorry I'm late, but I can explain. You'll see how unfair you're being if you'll only listen."

But Barb wasn't going to listen. She had put her hands over her ears. Her eyes had turned up, and white froth bubbled from her mouth as she began to scream.

Maris looked at her in horror. From upstairs came the sound of crying, Vicky calling out. "Mummy, Mummy!" Barb didn't hear. Her screams went on and on until Derek Forrest appeared in the doorway and made her stop.

CHAPTER FIFTEEN

The next day was first Saturday and they were supposed to be going to the farmer's market. Maris had been looking forward to it, but now she wasn't sure, after all that had happened last night. She got up and checked the children's room. They were already downstairs. Maris got dressed and followed reluctantly. She found them at the breakfast table, finishing their cereal, pink-cheeked with excitement, bursting to tell Maris all about the market.

"Are you sure we're going?" Maris asked.

They looked at her and then at each other, bewildered.

"I mean . . ." Maris stopped. "Where's your mum?"

"Having a lie-in," Vicky said. "She's feeling poorly."

"So who's going to take us?"

"Daddy, of course," Vicky said.

"He's upstairs right now, taking Mummy a cup of tea," Adam said.

"And when he comes down, he'll take us to the market," Vicky explained slowly, as if Maris were a baby.

"Oh," Maris said. She wouldn't have to face Barb just yet. She had been granted a reprieve.

She didn't mind that it was going to be the kids and her alone with Mr. Forrest. After last night, it would be hard to feel comfortable around Barb ever again. She was having a nervous breakdown, obviously. Tired All The Time, or TATT, was an excuse she made up to hide her true condition. It was ironic, Maris thought, that her mother had almost been right. She had hinted at something awful, not believing Barb simply needed a helping hand.

Mr. Forrest had called the doctor, who came out in the middle of the night, as no American doctor would, his suit pulled over his pajamas, to give Barb a shot. Maris had the feeling this wasn't the first time this had happened because Dr. Spears, a man with wild ginger hair and white eyebrows, seemed to know the ropes. He didn't have to be told where the master bedroom was. He went straight up the stairs.

Maris had thought she would feel uncomfortable being alone with Mr. Forrest in the sitting room, waiting until the doctor was finished. But for the first time, she was at ease. He had offered her strength and protection, putting his arms around her and giving her a fatherly hug. "I know, I know," he said, and told her to go wash her face while he made her a cup of tea.

Maris was horrified when she saw herself in the bathroom mirror. Black-ringed eyes stared; streaks of mascara ran down each cheek like long black tears. Smudged lipstick made her lips look bruised. In spots her face was a ghastly white, in others a lurid honey beige.

When Dr. Spears came down, he asked Maris if she needed something to help her sleep, but Maris refused. She drank the hot tea gratefully and said she would be all right.

"Keep an eye on her, then, Derek," the doctor said.

"She'll be quite safe with me."

And so she was. Maris and Mr. Forrest sat up until the wee hours, talking. She was tired but didn't want to sleep. He seemed to sense it. She was amazed at his range of knowledge, what he knew about animals, birds, trees, and flowers. He assured Maris that the animal in the woods had been either a fox or a dog, nothing more, and hardly dangerous. Foxes might be growing tamer but were still wary of encounters with people. A fox would have been curious but as frightened as she was. As for a lost or abandoned dog, no matter how hungry it was, it would have been timid and too suspicious to approach her. "There you were, terrified of each other," he said, and they laughed. In the sitting room, with lamps turned low and steaming cups of tea, the woods seemed remote, the fear a fantasy. Maris found herself telling him easily about what had happened with Brenda and her friends. "I've been a nuisance, I know but . . ."

"It seems to me you did the only sensible thing you could do. What matters is that you're back safe."

But Maris had wondered whether Barb would be as reasonable in the morning.

They went in Mr. Forrest's car, which was much bigger than Barb's mini and could hold all of them plus a load of groceries.

A woman was standing on the lawn in front of Milestones, a pair of garden shears in her hand. Mr. Forrest tooted and gave a wave as the car pulled out of the lane, but the woman didn't look up. She must have heard about Barb, Maris thought. As if reading her thoughts, Mr. Forrest said, "Not very friendly, is she?"

"She's a cow," Vicky said.

"None of that," Mr. Forrest reprimanded.

"That's what *you* said," Vicky persisted.

Adam deftly came to her rescue. "It's because of the dog, right, Dad?" Before his father could answer, Adam launched into a tale of neighborly disagreement. The people at Milestones once had a dog, he told Maris, which had been killed by a car. "They think it was our car, but it wasn't, right, Dad?"

Mr. Forrest shook his head. "Of course not."

"The trouble is they still pine for him," Vicky said. "His name was Spike."

"No, it wasn't," Adam argued.

"Why don't they get another dog?" Maris asked, but no one seemed inclined to give her an answer.

The market was in a town near Kelton. The main street was filled with stalls selling food and everything else under the sun: clothing, used furniture, books, records, broken-down electric appliances; it looked like a garage sale.

Mr. Forrest had a list of groceries. Maris liked the way he let Adam and Vicky take their time and help choose sausages and loaves of bread. Maris felt important, too, being asked advice on the week's menu.

"I'm afraid you may have to do more cooking than you bargained for," he said. "I hope you don't mind?"

"If you don't mind my cooking!"

They quickly filled up the two large plastic shopping bags. After they loaded the car, Mr. Forrest suggested a cup of tea, obviously part of the Saturday market ritual.

"Tell you what," he said when Adam and Vicky had finished their tea and cream buns. "Why don't you pop over to Mrs. Plum's stall and buy some sweets."

Their eyes widened. "Can we really?" they asked.

"Special treat today."

Maris laughed as they ran off. "Mrs. Plum?"

"She once volunteered to make phone calls to raise money and she got this old fellow on the line who was called Lemon. 'Hello, Mr. Lemon,' she said. 'This is Mrs. Plum.' He hung up on her." He smiled as Maris sputtered her tea.

"Will the kids be okay alone?" she asked, feeling she was neglecting her duties as an au pair.

"They know their way around."

She would have liked to ask him about Barb, but it probably wasn't the right time or place. He might have friends who would come in and overhear. He might not want to talk about his wife with her. She was a babysitter, not a real friend, no matter how nice he had been last night.

Friends. Now, that was odd. So far, Barb's only friends, if you could call them that, were the old dears who had come to tea, old ladies from a cooking club. Who were her real friends, people her own age? What about the mothers of kids who went to school with Adam and Vicky? What about people Mr. Forrest knew at work?

"Penny for your thoughts."

"I was just thinking . . ." But she couldn't say what she had been thinking of. "What do you do? I mean, your job, I never really found out."

He seemed amused. "Let's say computers." He caught sight of a man carrying an accordion past the tea shop. He began to tell her about him, how long he had been playing at all the markets in the vicinity.

He really is a nice man, Maris thought, sorry she had misjudged Mr. Forrest. His moods were no doubt because of Barb. Her illness must be a terrible strain. He had to put up with a lot. What would he do when Maris went home to the States?

She decided she'd try to help as much as possible and stop being so judgmental. She had wanted to prove something to her mother, that she was responsible. Well, the best way to do that was to just do it.

She felt his hand on hers and started at the touch, so warm and unexpected. He withdraw it, but she had felt something go through her, as if he had spoken to her with his touch and she reacted without thought, asking, "What?"

His eyes were quizzical. "Time to fetch the brats, what else?"

"Oh, yes," she stammered, rising from her chair and upsetting her teacup. "Sorry, how stupid — "

He touched her arm. "It was empty; no harm done."

She hadn't noticed before, had never looked at his hands so closely, so specifically; well, she had never felt them quite this way before and now wished she hadn't. In the moment before he removed his hand she saw the fingers, lying lightly against the bare flesh of her freckled arm. The same long graceful fingers that she had admired the day she met him. Only. Only something seemed wrong.

She looked away, afraid he would notice her staring. But he only smiled and picked up the bill to pay at the counter, then beckoned Maris into the sunlight. Adam and Vicky were running toward them, small paper sacks of candy clutched in their hands.

"Look what we got!" Adam said.

"She gave us extra mints," Vicky said, opening the bag and sticking her nose down into it. She proffered it to Maris. "They make you sneeze."

Laughing, Maris gave the bag an obliging sniff and then, to everyone's delight, sneezed.

"What a lovely family," a woman said as she moved past them into the tea shop. She nodded at the children and then to Maris. "You and your husband are very lucky."

"He's not . . ." Maris began. She felt her cheeks burning. But Mr. Forrest and the kids were bustling off toward the car. She followed, flustered and embarrassed. Deep down was a feeling she could not identify. Something like great happiness tinged with stark terror.

CHAPTER SIXTEEN

There were moments when she remembered the tea shop and the old woman's words and wondered if they were an omen.

But Barb had been sick for a long time, long before Maris came to England. It was foolish — no, egotistical — to think she could have done anything to undo what happened. Wasn't that what Mrs. Li always said? The only soul you could be responsible for was your own.

They had arrived home from the market in great spirits, singing nonsense songs, telling jokes.

"Why did the pig leave her husband?" Adam asked. "Why?"

"Because he was an old boar."

Maris forgot some of her apprehension about facing Barb and wasn't even thinking about her when they pulled up to the house and unloaded the car. Mr. Forrest said it was time for lunch, even though they had just eaten cream cakes. He got out cheese and apples and set the table himself.

Almost half an hour had passed before Maris remembered that Barb was still upstairs. She felt a guilty flush at having such a good time when the person she was supposed to be helping was feeling so bad.

"Should I go up and check on Barb?" she asked.

Mr. Forrest looked up from the apple he was deftly peeling and glanced at the clock, as if he, too, might be feeling guilty that so much time had passed before they gave Barb a thought.

"That's very kind of you," he said. "Why not bring her a cup of tea?"

Maris made the tea and arranged a tray. The children were finished with their cheese and fruit and wanted to come along, to tell Mummy all about the market. But as Maris started up the stairs, their father called them back.

"Let's wait until we see how Mummy is feeling," he said.

The bedroom door was shut. Maris tapped, but there was no answer. Barb was probably napping, but she'd welcome a cup of hot tea. It was doubtful she had even gone downstairs while they were at the market. Maris had to put the tea tray down to open the door. She peered in. The room was dim, lit only by the thin light of the bedside lamp. The room smelled strange. Maris had an incongruous vision of No. 2 lead pencils, the kind she used in grade school, the kind that smudged all over your paper.

It didn't look as if Barb was in bed. The sheets had been turned back; their riotous pattern of flowers were bright splotches of red and purple that looked as wet and shiny as freshly watered blooms in the light of the bedside lamp.

Maris put the tray down on a chest of drawers near the door and went across the room to open the drapes. Lamplight was depressing on such a nice day, could only make Barb feel worse.

She pulled the heavy lined velvet back and let in a wide band of sunlight. It spilled across the windowsill down to the floor and flowed with merciless brightness across the rug and onto the bed.

Maris almost laughed at her stupidity. There had never been any flowered sheets. They had always been white, bleached by the sun, hung on the outdoor line by Agnes. The laugh choked her, turned into a cough. Maris put her hand over her mouth, willing herself to swallow the bile that had rushed into her throat.

She swallowed hard and tried to call out to Mr. Forrest. Her voice creaked with terror, the cry nothing more than a whisper.

And then she was running down the staircase, her hands clenched into fists that would beat against his chest when he grabbed her to keep her from flying out the door.

It was only the children that brought her back to her senses. She heard them, in spite of the pounding of her heart, clamoring up the stairs behind her, and she spun around. Finding her voice at last, she yelled, "You don't want to go up there. You don't want to see."

She would never forget it. Barb's body lying at the side of the bed, splashed with those same mistaken red and purple blossoms, her hands neatly folded across her chest like a sleeping nun, her wrists sprung open, leaking blood like molten lava from the swollen cracks of her erupted flesh.

PART TWO

CHAPTER SEVENTEEN

On the morning of the inquest, Agnes was tidying the kitchen, doing the light housework that she normally refused to do. Since Monday, she had been breaking her rules, coming five days a week instead of three, helping with all the meals. She was the same dour woman as before, but Maris noticed her surreptitiously brushing tears from her eyes when she thought no one was looking.

"What's this lot doing in here?" she asked in the harsh voice Maris had come to recognize as bluster. She brandished her dustcloth at a bunch of papers inside a large cook pot that had been stored in the bottom of the kitchen cupboard.

"Recipes and stuff," Maris said, recognizing the

manila envelope Miss Flood had given to Barb the day of the tea party.

"Recipes! You better sort through and see if there's anything worth saving. I know that policeman said not to throw anything away, but he hardly meant us to keep every scrap of rubbish."

Maris took the stack from her. "Some of this is from her cooking club."

"What cooking club?"

"The one she and those old ladies belonged to."

Agnes looked down her nose. "You must be joking. Mrs. Forrest went in for Great Book discussions and such, not cookery."

Maris wasn't going to argue. She continued putting the breakfast dishes away. She had learned that the best way to keep things together was to catch them before they fell apart. Put things away, keep things neat. Discipline. It made the children feel better to stick to a routine, and a neat house cheered their father up. He acted hesitantly grateful that this burden had not fallen to him.

Finished, she sat down at the kitchen table and began to look through the pile of papers. They were what Maris had thought, the usual stuff you don't know what to do with: grocery receipts, outdated coupons, hints clipped from magazines. She supposed it was all right to throw them away. She glanced idly into the manila envelope. It took a few seconds for the contents to register. These were not recipes, these were newspaper and magazine articles and photocopied pages of books.

Maris looked up. Agnes had her head in the depths of the cupboard, scrubbing places neglected for years. If Agnes knew that Barb was interested in stuff like this, would she have handed it over so carelessly? More likely, Barb wanted to keep the stuff hidden but hadn't had time to find a better place. Holding the envelope open with her fingers, peering down without removing the pages, Maris read the name engraved on the paper that had been used for the photocopies: The Society for the Study of Lycanthropy. It wasn't a familiar word, but she read it with a shiver. And although the definition lurked at the far edges of her mind, there was a warning in the recognition. The old ladies had lied. Barb had kept it secret. Maris needed time to think about it.

"Oh, gosh," she said, looking at the clock. "I have to get ready."

There was a muffled acknowledgment from Agnes. Maris took the envelope to her room and put it under the mattress. She really did have to get dressed. Mr. Forrest would be coming to pick her up in half an hour. He had taken the children to some of his relatives in Selbridge to stay for the next few days. Originally, he had not wanted to send them away, believing they were better off in familiar surroundings. But when

Barb's mother, the children's grandmother, arrived, his plans changed. Dottie Rice reminded Maris of her own mother, someone who assumes she's in charge and knows all the answers to everyone's problems. Even the grief over her daughter's death could not soften her domineering attitude.

"My poor sweeties," she had said, smothering the children with kisses they did not return. She was an older version of Barb, but the pale hair was bleached and strawlike and the thinness revealed slack skin on angular bones. She had none of Barb's warmth. Adam and Vicky remained quietly aloof, thanking her politely when she presented them with bags of American candy and plastic toys. "They can't stay in this living trauma!" she admonished. "Everything reminds them of their mother. They need a break." Mrs. Rice announced her plan to take Adam and Vicky back home to America with her.

Maris had a bad moment then, seeing herself packed up and sent away, too, back to her mother, the summer over before it began. She stared hard at Derek Forrest, willing him to put up a fight.

But she need not have worried. Derek Forrest was firm. The children would stay in England with him. Later on, they might come for a visit. At Christmas, perhaps.

This put Mrs. Rice's nose out of joint. She frowned

and said, "We'll see," and Maris could almost feel her rearming.

But Mrs. Rice wasn't the only threat.

"I want you on the next plane out of there!" her mother ordered when she phoned. Maris had not bothered to let her know about Barb's death, but, of course, Mrs. Rice had told her.

"I can't," Maris said feebly, unprepared.

"Don't worry, they'll change your ticket. They'll have to under the circumstances."

"It's not that." Maris tried to keep her voice steady. "I have to stay here because of the inquest. To give evidence."

"That's ridiculous! We're not talking murder. What evidence?"

"I found her body; I have to testify."

"They can't make you do that. You're only a child."

"I want to do it."

"I won't allow it."

But Maris knew there was nothing her mother could do. The police had been very specific. She was expected to tell the court what she had seen. The inquest won her a reprieve.

"Afterwards, then. Fly back with Dottie and the kids."

"Dottie's going to St. Louis. And the kids are staying here."

"That's not what I heard, but it's beside the point. You can't stay there with a man. Unchaperoned!"

"Mr. Forrest needs help now more than ever."

Her mother laughed. "Don't be ridiculous."

"He has no one else."

"Look, Maris, why do I have to repeat myself? Mrs. Rice is taking custody of the children and Mr. Forrest will have to fend for himself."

Maris tried to stay calm. Home had been far away in the future; she hadn't given it much thought. Now, with her mother's voice harping in her ear, she realized how much she dreaded it. "Big change," Mrs. Li had said. That's what Maris wanted, with all her heart, a big change. Never to go back.

"Suicide, for heaven's sake," her mother was ranting. "It's not a proper environment."

Maybe things were a little weird, Maris thought. But if she could handle finding Barb's body, she could handle whatever else came along. She liked herself now. This new Maris was someone of importance. She was going to testify at an inquest. People wanted to hear what she had to say.

"Bye, Mom." She had hung up abruptly.

She took care dressing now. A conservative look was best. A not-too-short skirt and a loose blouse. There must be no question of her being capable and mature, a person needed in the Forrest household.

*   *   *

The inquest went mostly as Derek Forrest had said it would. He testified first. Afterward came remarks from the police and ambulance attendants. Then it was Maris's turn. As she walked to the front of the courtroom, her knees threatened to shake. She took a deep breath. In what she hoped was an unwavering and confident voice, she recounted the events of that Saturday morning. Her voice trembled only a little when she got to the part of actually discovering Barb's body. But she was dismayed that when she tried to be specific about the wounds, she began to cry.

Mrs. Rice patted her hand when she sat down again. "You did a good job, dear." The words did not soften Maris's heart.

Dr. Spears testified that he had been treating Barbara Forrest for depression for the past year and that he had many times recommended a psychiatrist, advice she refused to take. He had prescribed antidepressants, but he had no way of being certain that she actually took the medication on a regular basis.

Then it was Agnes's turn. She came forward looking as formidable as ever, with a stern face and haughty shoulders. But her hands, folding and unfolding a damp handkerchief, belied her outward bravado. Maris thought there was something of the look of a scared rabbit in her eyes, which she tried to hide by looking down. When questioned, she agreed that Mrs. Forrest had been depressed. Unexpectedly, she launched into a vicious attack, blaming Mr. Forrest and Dr. Spears for being the cause. She was asked to enlighten the court with something more specific.

"Her husband wanted her to snap out of it, as if it were as easy as snapping your fingers." Agnes demonstrated. "But he did nothing to help her. And whatever the doctor was giving her just made her worse, not better."

"That is a serious accusation," Agnes was warned. "Are you saying that Dr. Spears administered something other than a legally prescribed medication?"

Agnes hedged and the court was reminded that the forensics report had shown the traces of tricyclic antidepressants in Mrs. Forrest's bloodstream to be congruent with the doses Dr. Spears had prescribed, the prescriptions of which Mrs. Forrest had regularly filled at the Kelton chemist. Agnes seemed about to protest. But when she looked up, she caught Derek Forrest's eye and her voice dried up.

Mrs. Rice was agitated when it was her turn to speak. "I had not seen my daughter in more than a year. I knew she was having problems, but if this means there's a chance her death wasn't suicide . . ."

The judge reminded Mrs. Rice that although the wrist wounds were of a particularly gory nature, it had been shown conclusively that they had been made by Mrs. Forrest's own teeth. The blood and flesh found in the mouth was further proof, unpleasant as it was.

"But if someone drove her to do it . . ." Mrs. Rice glared at her son-in-law and Dr. Spears. Maris's heart thumped. Was this how she planned to get custody of the children?

"There is also the note, written in her own hand," said the judge. He was calm and sympathetic toward Mrs. Rice, but adamant. The verdict was death by suicide.

When they came out of the courthouse, the weather had changed. Gloomy rain fell from a solemn sky. Mr. Forrest ran for the car while Maris and Mrs. Rice stood in the shelter of the doorway.

"Can you believe it?" Mrs. Rice said. "Nobody wants to do anything."

The proceedings had upset Maris more than she would have imagined. Hearing about how Barb had actually torn her veins with her teeth, how she had swallowed chunks of her own flesh. It wasn't something she wanted to think about anymore. "Do what?" she asked.

"Arrest somebody!" Mrs. Rice shouted as the car arrived. She got in next to Derek and launched again into her campaign about the children coming to live with her.

"We've already agreed on that, Dottie."

"I agreed before I heard what Agnes had to say."

"Barb had a lot of problems."

"And who gave her those problems?" Mrs. Rice asked archly.

He looked at her.

Mrs. Rice was indignant. "Don't think I'm letting it end here, because I'm not. I don't care what the verdict was today. Only someone completely insane would . . . would bite themselves to death. And my daughter was not insane."

"Her letter said she didn't want to go on living," Derek said. "It was depression, not insanity."

"But why?" Mrs. Rice cried. "What could have been so awful in her life that she couldn't face living anymore?"

Mrs. Rice's plans were to go through all Barb's stuff. It was a reasonable request, but after having seen the contents of the manila envelope, Maris wished she could search the room first. Agnes's testimony and Mrs. Rice's threats had disturbed her. If Derek were implicated in Barb's death, it would make things easier for Mrs. Rice. She'd take the children away and Maris would have to go home. But if Maris could find something weird, to show Barb was crazy after all, then nobody could blame Derek.

The information in the envelope wasn't good enough. It could be information for the book discussions Agnes said Barb liked, even though lycanthropy was a fancy name for turning into werewolves, as Maris had found in the dictionary. She only hoped there was more in Barb's room. There had to be. Otherwise, why would the old ladies and Barb have lied and kept it so secret? Maris had to get there first. If Mrs. Rice found anything, she'd throw it out. More and more, she was making Barb sound like a saint.

Worse, she was getting Agnes on her side. They acted chummy together. Maris wished she could fire Agnes. Agnes wasn't needed anymore. Maris could handle everything.

She calculated. Derek would pick the kids up from Selbridge on Wednesday. The funeral was Thursday. Mrs. Rice was leaving Monday. Maris didn't trust her an inch. She kept going through the children's dresser drawers, sorting out their clothes. She was capable of anything, even kidnapping the children.

It was this thought that gave Maris the courage to speak to Derek Forrest. She found him alone in the garden, reading a newspaper. They were well out of earshot of anybody else.

He looked at her inquiringly. Facing him, she felt less sure, but she went ahead anyway. "I was wondering. Do Adam and Vicky have passports?"

He gave a tired smile. "Don't tell me you want to take them to America, too?"

"Well, I know this is going to sound strange, but Barb's mother is up to something. She and Agnes are making plans against you."

"Isn't that a bit melodramatic?"

She tried not to show her disappointment or impatience. "I'm serious, Mr. Forrest. Mrs. Rice could kidnap the kids. In America, it happens all the time."

He raised an eyebrow. "Grandmothers kidnapping grandchildren?"

"Really. I've seen it on television. Please don't make fun of me."

"I'm sorry, I didn't mean to sound flippant. But I'm tired of all this. Dottie has done nothing but argue in spite of the fact that we agreed to wait until Christmas. I don't know what's got into her."

"She thinks you caused Barb's death." Maris blurted the words without thinking and held her breath. But when he only gave her a sad stare and looked back down at the newspaper, she was glad she had said it.

She almost wished it would happen. If Mrs. Rice took the kids while he was at work, Maris would be the only one who could stop her. This would show him she knew what she was talking about.

"It's unlikely that Mrs. Rice would go to extremes," he was saying. "But if it will make you feel better, I'll put the childrens' passports in a safe place."

Maris couldn't tell if he was being sarcastic. She wasn't sure if she had been dismissed. But he spoke again. "It's unusual for them to even have passports." His face grew dark as he looked off into the garden. "We were planning a trip abroad." He shook himself and looked back at her. "Adam and Victoria have been through enough. They don't need any more traumas, as Dottie calls them. I suppose I shouldn't be saying this to you, but I'm not very fond of her."

"I've known people like her. I understand."

His eyes narrowed, warm honey brown glinting gray. "Yes, well . . ." He picked up the newspaper again.

Maris didn't want the conversation to end. "Where were you going? On your trip?"

"Where? Oh, someplace in the Balkans. Maybe Russia."

"Oh." It wasn't what she had expected.

"The mountains are beautiful there. I wanted to see the steppes. Great vast loneliness. No humans for miles."

There was a yearning pensiveness in his voice that pinched Maris with jealousy.

"It might have helped heal the rift between us. I'm sure even you saw it was there. But it wasn't always."

The jealousy hurt. Almost made her angry. But the rift could never be healed now, could it?

"Excuse me for going on in this maudlin way."

"I don't think it's maudlin to feel sad about not being able to go there," Maris said gently.

"Well, who knows? Maybe it's still a possibility. My life hasn't ended."

If he got away from here, Maris thought, he'd get away from all these reminders of Barb. She imagined herself going away with him and the children. A family. All of them together. She wanted to be a person important enough for him to care whether she stayed here or went home. And she was tired of being an in-between. Agnes and Mrs. Rice were on one side, Mr. Forrest and the kids on another. She wanted to belong in the family. There had never been any kind of family feeling at home. In Sophie's house you knew they were a family. They stuck together, they liked each other, there was this warm feeling around them. It was when she had gone to Sophie's that she noticed the atmosphere in her own home most. Cold. Her mother was businesslike if she wasn't yelling. Her mother never patted her cheek the way Sophie's mother did, and said she was her sweet girl.

Maris realized she had a limited time to find a way into the Forrest solidarity. She had to find the key that would let her in, and soon. Otherwise, her mother would do something to mess everything up.

"Well, I'll be getting back to the house," Maris said, when Mr. Forrest said nothing more. She turned away reluctantly, but she could see he wanted to be left alone.

"Maris?" he called out. "Please don't address me as

Mr. Forrest in such a formal way. You never did it with Barbara."

"Well, I just felt . . ."

"Call me Derek, won't you?"

She hoped he was not mocking her. "Of course. Derek."

Walking back to the house, she was acutely aware of his eyes on her. She tried to walk slowly, hiding and cherishing the excitement that made her want to run around and shout.

Maris one. Mrs. Rice nil.

Only five more days to go.

CHAPTER EIGHTEEN

The scream rang in her ears. A dream scream or real? She listened and heard nothing but the memory of it. The house seemed quiet. A nightmare, although she couldn't remember what she had been dreaming about. Just a dream.

And then came the sound of whimpering. Across the hall, the children. Maris jumped out of bed and hurried to them, wanting to get there before Dottie Rice heard and came upstairs from the sitting room where she was sleeping on the Hide-A-Bed.

"Adam, Vicky, what's the matter?"

It was Vicky who was whimpering, huddled in her bed like a little ball. Adam was at the window, leaning out into the night.

"Adam, what are you doing?"

"Didn't you hear it?"

So it hadn't been a dream. "Yes, I think so."

He turned away from the window. His face was drawn and pale. The resemblance to his mother was startling.

"I think something died," he said. His voice was matter-of-fact, but he looked shaken.

"Oh, come on," Maris said, hugging him and leading him away from the window. "Why should you think that?"

"Bad things happen here sometimes."

"What kind of bad things?"

Adam glanced toward Vicky. He was only a child, but the meaning was unmistakably protective. Don't talk in front of his little sister.

They couldn't have talked anyway because at that moment Mrs. Rice burst into the room. "What's going on?" she demanded, flicking the wall switch to the overhead light, changing the room's soft night-light glow into a blinding artificial blaze.

"Nothing's going on," Maris said, blinking. "Vicky had a bad dream. I'm taking care of her."

Frowning, looking like a scarecrow in her long robe and disheveled strawlike hair, Mrs. Rice looked around the room suspiciously. "Everything is not fine. Some animal screeching its head off wakes me up and then I hear the children crying and to top it off, he isn't even here."

Adam had climbed back into his bed and pulled up the sheet. Vicky was still curled into her protective ball, but she had stopped crying.

Maris stood in front of the beds, shielding the children, blocking Mrs. Rice's way. "Who's not here?"

"Their father! I looked in his room and the bed is empty."

Maris struggled to get herself together. "Well . . . so what? I mean, maybe he's downstairs or in the garden." What nerve, barging into Derek's bedroom.

"At a time like this?"

Maris didn't know if she meant it was so late at night or because Barb had died. She didn't know what to do with Mrs. Rice at that moment. She just felt she must protect the kids, keep Mrs. Rice from snatching them up and running off.

"He's probably sitting outside in the garden."

"He's not in the garden. I looked when I was trying to see what kind of animal was making that god-awful noise. He must have gone out. Without telling me. It's unbelievable."

Maris felt a tremor of fear. She wanted him back. She needed him back. "Is the car gone?"

This hadn't occurred to Mrs. Rice. She was momentarily flustered. Maris wasn't going to be the one to go and see. She wasn't leaving the children alone with

Mrs. Rice for a minute. "Go check on the car and I'll get the kids back to sleep."

Mrs. Rice rushed out and Maris quickly turned the overhead light off.

"Why does she have to be our granny?" Vicky asked in a tiny voice. "I don't want her to be our granny."

Adam looked up at Maris. "We don't have to go to America with her, do we?"

"Not if I can help it."

"Good. We want you, not her, don't we, Vicky?"

"Yes, we want you, Maris. And Daddy. Only you and Daddy, now that Mummy's not here anymore."

Maris sat down on Adam's bed. "Then let me tell you something, okay? It's very important that you don't let Mrs. Rice take you anywhere. Don't get in a taxi with her or anything. Don't let her take you with her. Promise?"

Vicky nodded, wide-eyed.

"But what if she makes us?" Adam asked.

"Don't let her. Yell, run away, make a fuss. Hide if you have to." She could see they were getting worried. "Look, I'll be here. I won't let her do anything to you."

"Good," Vicky said.

"Now you guys go back to sleep, okay?"

Obediently, they closed their eyes. But as Maris went to the door, Adam said, "If she does get us, will you take care of MacDuff?"

"She's not going to get you, Adam."

"But if she does, could you be sure to take care of MacDuff? Make sure the cage is locked?"

"Yes, I will. But you don't have to worry."

"Never leave the lock off," Adam persisted.

"Never," Vicky echoed. "Or something will come and eat him up."

"Shut up, Vicky," Adam said.

Maris wished she could ask him more about the bad things, but she thought it was best to leave it until morning. Right now she wanted to find Derek.

When she came downstairs, Mrs. Rice was in the kitchen. Again she had switched on the overhead light, turning the windows into mirrors. Maris felt exposed.

"He's nowhere," Mrs. Rice said. "I'm making tea. Sit down."

"Is the car gone?"

Grudgingly, Mrs. Rice admitted both cars were still parked outside.

"So okay," Maris said, flooded with relief. "What's the problem?"

"If he's not here, where is he?"

"Taking a walk?"

"That's crazy. You don't take a walk in the middle of the night."

"Why not?" It was just like her mother. Telling people what they could and couldn't do.

"Because . . ." Mrs. Rice hesitated. "Because he left his children all alone." This idea appealed to her and she got up steam. "It's obvious he can't cope. A man who leaves his children alone in the middle of the night isn't a responsible father."

Maris smiled. "But he didn't leave them alone. He left them with us."

Mrs. Rice faltered for a moment, then waved Maris's objections away. "That's beside the point."

Maris heard herself say, coldly, "It won't work. You won't get them." She hadn't planned to let her feelings out in the open. Now she had given herself away. Mrs. Rice narrowed her eyes. It was out-and-out war between them.

"Really? How do you know? I've already started the ball rolling with the lawyers. And I have Agnes to back me up. So there's nothing you can do about it." She snapped the kettle off and poured boiling water into her cup. She looked up at the ceiling and laughed. "Why am I talking to you anyway? You're just a baby yourself."

"I'm not a baby!" Maris said angrily. "And there are things I can do."

Mrs. Rice stirred the tea and looked at her with scorn. "Sweetie, you're way out of line."

"So are you. You have no right to take Derek's kids away from him."

"Oh, so it's Derek now."

Maris blanched. She was only giving Mrs. Rice more ammunition. She had to keep her mouth shut. But it was hard, when she wanted to scream.

"I called them both by their first names. Barb asked me to. Barb didn't mind. Barb was the one who couldn't take care of her kids. Barb — "

"Please, leave my poor Barbara out of this." Her eyes puddled up and she took a tissue out of her pocket. "My sweet innocent daughter."

Maris couldn't help herself. There was a storm building up inside her. Mrs. Rice, her mother, they were interchangeable. "She wasn't so sweet and innocent. I know things about her you don't know."

"There's nothing — "

"Oh, yes, there is. Barb was into . . . stuff. . . ." Maris knew she shouldn't keep talking, but she couldn't stop herself. The revenge was too sweet. "She was into witchcraft."

"You little bitch!" Mrs. Rice raised her hand and Maris flinched. But then there was another hand, holding Mrs. Rice back. Maris could smell him before she even saw him, a scent that was becoming her talisman, recognition.

"That's enough, Dottie."

Mrs. Rice pulled away, spilling the tea, the cup smashing on the tile floor. "Where the hell have you been?"

"I didn't think I could sleep. I went walking on the

lane," Derek said quietly. He moved Mrs. Rice away from the broken cup. "Sit down. You're upset. You'll cut yourself."

"You're damn right I'm upset. If you could have heard what this little . . . this nasty . . ."

Maris's heart pounded. Had Derek heard what she had said? Would he be on her side, glad that she found out about Barb, or look on it as a betrayal?

He was clearing up the broken china. She knelt down to help. "Never mind, Maris," he said. His voice sounded cold. His hand brushed against hers and she drew back and stood up quickly, as if she had been burned.

"It's time for bed," Mrs. Rice said. Her face was pinched. "I'm speaking to you, Maris."

Maris stared at Derek and he looked back, holding the dustpan full of broken shards. His eyes were like pinpoints of moonlight. His skin glowed. His hair was damp, as if he had been running. She could see the sweat had soaked through his shirt, staining the underarms.

"It's a good idea for all of us," he said.

"The children were upset," Dottie Rice said. "I don't think — "

"I'm sure Maris saw to them," Derek said. "Didn't you, Maris?"

"I went up as soon as I heard them," Dottie Rice persisted.

"Good night," Derek said. He put his hand on Maris's arm. "Good night."

She looked down at his fingers. She saw what she had seen that time in the tea shop. The length was all wrong. She stopped herself from wanting to count them.

"I won't get a wink of sleep," Dottie Rice said, "listening for my poor girl's babies."

Maris turned and ran up the stairs. She didn't think she could stand another moment of that woman's voice.

In her room, she thought about how Derek had put his hand on her arm when saying good night. She had thought his words cold, and then that friendly gesture. It made her head ache, trying to figure things out. And the argument with Dottie — that had reminded her of old times! Just like arguing with her mother. If only Dottie would just . . . what? Disappear. Drop dead.

Maris sat down on her bed and thought about Derek's hand on her arm. Something was wrong, but not just about the length of his fingers. She'd noticed that. They just didn't seem normal. But something else. When he had been bending down to sweep up the broken cup. The label on the collar of his shirt. The seams.

Weird. But he had been wearing his shirt inside out.

CHAPTER NINETEEN

It was a reprimand; you couldn't call it anything else. Maris felt like a child being scolded.

"I couldn't help overhearing what you said to Mrs. Rice last night. Accusations like those are serious. It isn't wise to talk about things you don't understand."

"I didn't mean anything."

"You must have meant something. Why tell such lies about Barbara?"

Lies? He thought they were lies. He didn't know about the Society for the Study of Lycanthropy. Barb had kept it a secret.

"But Mrs. Rice thinks Barb was wonderful and you're not. She's getting lawyers to give her custody of the children."

Derek gave her a patient smile, the kind of smile you give a stupid kid, the kind of sarcastic smile her mother used to give her. "I'm sure I can handle anything Mrs. Rice is planning. But I don't think it's your worry, Maris. You're here to look after Adam and Victoria. Please limit yourself to that, won't you, and let me take care of lawyers and Mrs. Rice."

"But that's the point. I am looking after the kids! You don't believe me. You don't understand what she's going to do."

"Maris, please. This has been a strain on all of us. Mrs. Rice will be leaving in a few days. Let's just get on with life and forget the melodrama."

He thought she was being hysterical. She felt completely let down. What about all that stuff yesterday, asking her to call him Derek? What about that look last night, and touching her hand? He must have felt something for her. She wanted to shake him, she was so angry. And at the same time she wanted to tell him it was all right. But he got up from the chair behind the desk. She had been summoned and now she was dismissed. He was going to his office, to catch up on things.

"Take the children for a walk. They need exercise. Don't let them get moody." Orders to the au pair.

She called Adam and Vicky and suggested they walk to the village, the way they had before. It seemed years ago now. It would tire them out. They had been very mopey, and Vicky was inclined to burst into tears at anything that reminded her of her mother.

"Got some money for candy?" Maris asked, and they grew a little more enthusiastic.

"Where are you going?" Mrs. Rice wanted to know.

"To the Parade," Vicky said.

"There's a parade? Where is it?" Mrs. Rice asked.

Adam and Vicky laughed, stopped themselves, looked at Maris, and saw she was laughing, too.

"It's not a parade like people marching," Adam explained. "It's what you call the shops."

Mrs. Rice perked up. "Shops? Wait. I'll be ready in a few minutes."

"But we don't want you to come," Vicky blurted out.

Mrs. Rice looked appalled and Vicky went very red in the face.

"What she means is that we're walking, Mrs. Rice," Maris said. "It's a very long way to the village and Vicky thought you wouldn't want to walk that far."

Adam looked relieved and took Maris's hand and held it. Vicky moved closer to her. Mrs. Rice stared at them. "No problem. We'll take the car."

"Derek . . . Mr. Forrest . . . is using it to go to his office."

"The other car. Barbara's car," Mrs. Rice said. And then, as if she read Maris's mind, "I'm sure I can manage to drive on the left."

Maris tried to make her voice sweet. "Mr. Forrest wanted the children to get some exercise. It's better if we walk."

The older woman shrugged. "Okay. We'll walk."

There was nothing Maris could do about it. They had to wait while Dottie Rice changed to slacks and a pair of Nikes.

They started out, and the kids dragged, no longer enthusiastic, probably thinking their grandmother would have something to say about how much candy they could or could not buy.

"Come on, don't mope." Mrs. Rice stepped out, setting a lively pace. "Exercise should be exercise."

She kept it up for five minutes and then Maris noticed perspiration breaking out on her brow.

"Do you need to slow down?" Maris asked.

"That's a good idea. The kids really can't keep up with their small legs, can they?" Mrs. Rice laughed breathlessly. "In fact, let's give them a rest a minute."

Maris thought at this rate, they'd never get to the village.

Dottie Rice sprawled onto the grass and rummaged in the canvas purse she was carrying over her arm. She pulled out a brown prescription container.

"Anything wrong?" Maris asked.

"Oh, it's nothing. I have a slight irregular heart-beat. Perfectly benign but annoying. I forgot to take one this morning. No big deal," she said offhandedly as she put a small blue pill into her palm.

"Don't you need some water?"

Mrs. Rice shook her head and swallowed. "They're tiny. Anyway, I trained myself, just in case I had to take one . . . at a time like this." She looked around as if just noticing the countryside. "How pretty." She breathed in deeply. "You know, Maris, we don't have to be enemies. How did we get into that argument last night? Seems silly now, doesn't it?"

Maris felt awkward. She probably meant it, but Maris didn't feel like making up.

Mrs. Rice smiled. "After all, we're both concerned about the same thing."

Adam and Vicky were sitting cross-legged nearby. They were studying some insect they'd caught, but Maris knew they were listening to every word.

"I guess so," Maris said. "It will be nice for you to see the kids at Christmas."

Mrs. Rice put the pill container back into her purse. "Sure . . . Christmas." She looked over at the children. "You'll like Christmas in St. Louis. A lot different from here."

"How different?" Vicky asked suspiciously.

"Snow. Piles of snow to build snowmen with. I bet you never saw a snowman!"

Vicky put on her disgusted look, but Adam said diplomatically, "Actually, I made one once. Vicky was littler. We went on holiday up north."

"Mummy didn't like it," Vicky said.

"Dad wanted to see the hills. He likes places where no one lives. He says he wishes he could live way up in the mountains and hunt for all our food."

Oh, shut up, Adam, please, Maris thought. Don't tell all the family secrets. She was sure the wheels were turning in Mrs. Rice's brain.

"You know," Mrs. Rice said, "I think I will go back to the house. I feel a little tired. You have yourselves a real good time. It's a beautiful day."

They watched her walk off. The atmosphere immediately lightened. Adam and Vicky ran ahead, challenging each other to a race.

As it turned out, it wasn't a beautiful day after all. Before they reached the shops, the sky darkened and a hard rain drenched them. They felt lucky to see the return bus from Banfield coming down the road. They hailed it and got on, and so they came back to the house a whole lot earlier than they should have.

Maris had run ahead after they got off the bus, not as delighted as Adam and Vicky with getting soaked. As she stepped through the doorway, she heard Dottie Rice speaking on the telephone. To her lawyer, obviously. Talking about getting an injunction against Derek. Incompetent as a father, taking small children to a crematorium and letting them see their mother's coffin! Dangerous, too. Just last night he had almost beaten her up. And the girl. "There's something fishy going on, if you ask me. I don't like to insinuate, but for all I know, they're sleeping together. I tell you, we have to do this quickly and we have to do it right."

The children, prolonging the fun, had just come up, splashing their feet in the puddles. Maris stepped out the door again and told them to stop and took their hands.

"Hey, we're back!" she called out as they came in the door together.

Mrs. Rice turned, replacing the phone in its cradle. "Oh, you poor things, you must be drenched. I'll make some hot tea."

"That'll be nice," Maris said, forcing herself to smile. Two could play the same game, she thought.

The trouble was, time was running out. She had to find out about Barb pretty soon. And she had to find out about Mrs. Rice's plans. Snake in the grass, her mother used to say about people she didn't trust. It was an expression that fit Dottie Rice perfectly.

CHAPTER TWENTY

The rain continued, making the next morning miserable. Maris looked out the window and saw a magpie. "One magpie. Don't look," Vicky had warned. Maris turned away and went back and sat on her unmade bed, turning Mrs. Li's Chinese ball around and around in her hands. She didn't need one magpie, she needed luck.

"Some days lucky, some days not," Mrs. Li always said. She could look at a whole pan of fried rice that her son had spilled on the floor and laugh. "This one unlucky day!"

Maris turned her gaze to the papers spread out on the bed, as if in the last few minutes they had somehow changed and would now offer a way to get the information she needed.

The Society for the Study of Lycanthropy was in Yorkshire. Obviously too far away to visit, and she'd never get any real information by phone.

That was insurmountable problem number one. Number two was how to get proof of Mrs. Rice's plans. Maris could hardly walk into the solicitor's office and demand copies of the files.

Think of the good side, she told herself. She had, since yesterday, accomplished one thing. She had found out the name of Mrs. Rice's lawyer. It had been written on the notepad the woman kept in her address book. Only a name and a phone number. But Maris had looked it up in the county directory to make sure.

"Maris? You still in bed?" Mrs. Rice's strident voice came from downstairs.

"I'll be there in a minute."

She stuffed the papers back into the manila envelope and shoved it under the mattress.

Dottie Rice was sitting at the kitchen table, drinking decaffeinated coffee. She insisted on decaffeinated, she said, otherwise she got jittery. Maybe it wasn't good for her heart, Maris thought. Could a woman with heart trouble get custody of little kids?

Maris put the kettle back on the stove and got the bread out to make herself tea and toast.

"Your mother called last night."

"What?"

"I said your mother called. She's made arrangements for your ticket back."

"What?"

"Maris, are you deaf or something?"

"Why didn't she talk to me?"

"She didn't want to speak to you. She told me you'd only get into another argument and she trusted me to be sure you got on the plane. All of us can go to the airport together."

"All of us?" Through the window, she saw Adam and Vicky playing with MacDuff. She wondered if Mrs. Rice planned to kidnap the rabbit, too. Damn! If only there was a way to get the proof.

Mrs. Rice stirred her coffee. "You and I can go together. For heaven's sake, what's the matter with you this morning?"

"I don't know."

"Well, I think I do. You need to be around people your own age. It'll do you good to get back to your friends."

Friends. The word hung in the air between them. But Maris wasn't thinking about Sophie or anyone at home. Perhaps there was a way after all, one that had been sitting right under her nose.

"I have friends here."

Mrs. Rice laughed. "Where are they? Hiding in the woodwork?"

"In Kelton. Barb introduced me to them. She wanted me to go out and have fun."

Mrs. Rice's eyes grew misty. "Yes, she would do that, wouldn't she? Well, why haven't you been seeing them?"

Maris looked down and toyed with the toast crusts. "I didn't think it was right, you know, with everything happening."

"Nonsense. It would do you good."

"I thought you'd get mad."

"Dear, I told you before, we're not enemies."

Maris smiled, sickly sweet. "Thanks."

She finished her toast and took her dirty plate to the sink. "Oh, when are we supposed to be leaving?"

"Next Friday. That's the only flight your mother could get you on and I decided I needed a few more days with the children anyway."

Give you more time for your arrangements, Maris thought. "Well, I guess I don't have to start packing today."

"Relax a little. Why not call these friends and get together to say good-bye?"

Maris could think of nothing she'd rather do less than get together with Brenda and her pals. "That's a good idea."

"Give them a call."

"I will."

Since it was Saturday, Brenda Finmore wouldn't be

at work. Maris got her home number from directory inquiries. She waited until Mrs. Rice went outside with the children before she called.

Brenda answered, sounding bored.

"Hi. It's me, Maris."

"Oh. Well?"

"Thanks for ratting on me. Why'd you phone Barb and tell her about the taxi?"

"I was worried about you."

"No, you weren't."

"Okay, okay. I was covering myself. I just wanted to make sure you got home. Kerry's no angel. I didn't need Gran on my back."

"Well, forget it. I was really calling about your grandmother anyway. I forgot her last name and I need her address and phone number."

"What do you want with my gran?"

"Not me. Barb's mother wants to send her a letter or something."

"Why don't you just ask Barb, then?"

"You don't know Barb committed suicide?"

"You're joking!"

"Yeah, I always joke about things like that."

"Crikey, when did it happen?"

"Last week. So do you have the number?"

Brenda gave her the information about Ethel Dunkley. "Look, do you want to go out again? Kerry was asking about you."

Kerry. That seemed like a million light-years ago. Compared to Derek Forrest, Kerry seemed silly and childish.

"I don't think right now."

"Sometime?"

"Sure."

"Cheers, then."

"Cheers."

CHAPTER TWENTY-ONE

Mrs. Dunkley was delighted to hear from Maris and invited her to tea on Sunday. "So sad about Barbara," she said, and Maris wondered again why there had been no friends or family at the short service before Barb was cremated. Of course, Maris hadn't said anything about the old ladies to Derek and he had not mentioned them himself.

Dottie Rice said she'd be glad to drive Maris to Elsmere, a little village on the outskirts of Kelton. But Derek could not understand why Maris would want to see Brenda again. "Wasn't she the girl who gave you such a bad time?"

"It was her friends' idea of a joke. It's just the two of us this time. No pubs." She hoped he wouldn't question her further, asking for details that she didn't want to explain in front of Dottie Rice. But it was Mrs. Rice who prevented that.

"She's going to see people her own age," she said. "And it's about time, too. You don't know anything about raising children, Derek."

He ignored her. "Maris, I expect you home early this time," he said. Maris wished there were more to his concern than fatherly interest. Well, wait until she presented him with proof.

Maris gave her grudging admiration when Mrs. Rice found Elsmere just by looking at a map. Mrs. Dunkley lived in a garden flat: a small apartment in a larger house. Maris waved good-bye and went through a garden full of flowers to get to the entrance at the back.

She needn't have worried about how she would bring up the Society for the Study of Lycanthropy. As soon as she came through the door, she noticed there were pictures of wolves all over the place, photographs and drawings. In some the wolves looked like big friendly dogs. In others, they were menacing, fierce.

Mrs. Dunkley picked up one of the framed pictures. "Do you like my collection? Some people don't take kindly to wolves."

"It's . . . unusual," Maris stammered. Bookshelves ran across one entire wall and were crammed full.

"I've never seen so many books."

Mrs. Dunkley laughed. "All of this is simply a drop

in the bucket. There's so much we don't know."

"About what?"

"Oh, dear, here I am waffling on and I haven't even offered you a cup of tea. Sit down, dear, and I'll bring it in."

The old lady disappeared into the kitchen. Maris went to the bookshelves and began snooping. There were books on all kinds of strange subjects: shamanism, witchcraft, and a good many on lycanthropy. Maris pulled one out. It showed pictures of wolves with human faces.

"Interesting, isn't it, dear?" Mrs. Dunkley asked from the doorway. She swept papers and more books aside before there was room to put the tea tray down on a table.

"This looks so . . . serious. Scientific. As if werewolves were real." Some of the illustrations were frightening. Maris didn't want to look at them too long.

"But, my dear, it's quite true. People can indeed turn themselves into a wide variety of animals. It's called shapeshifting. Your American Indians were quite good at it."

Mrs. Dunkley sat on a burgundy velvet loveseat and poured out the tea.

"But werewolves can't be real," Maris persisted. She had expected to find proof, but not so blatantly. It made her uneasy. If Mrs. Dunkley turned out to be totally crazy, she'd be no help at all.

"Not werewolves the way you mean. Not those creatures one sees in films, walking on their hind legs and tearing out people's throats. I'm talking about people who turn into real wolves. Wolves who act like wolves." She gestured toward her pictures. "See for yourself how beautiful they are. Lovely animals, badly maligned."

"But you . . . you've never seen one?"

Mrs. Dunkley peered at her over the rim of the teacup. "My dear, what's on your mind?"

Maris shifted uneasily. "I don't understand."

"Come, come, this is not a purely social call, is it?"

Maris felt embarrassed being caught. "Well, no," she admitted. "It's just that I found the stuff you gave Barb, pretending it was recipes. I was curious. I wondered if I should keep it secret, you know, from her mother and — "

Mrs. Dunkley, looking fierce, broke in. "People don't understand. They get it into their heads that it's witchcraft, dealings with the devil. Utter rubbish! Gladys and I are interested not only from an academic standpoint. We want to protect those who can change. And, as you might have guessed, dear Barbara had a more personal interest."

"Personal? You don't mean she thought she was one?"

Mrs. Dunkley gave her a hard stare. "Barbara is dead. Let her secrets lie with her."

"But Mrs. Dunkley . . . I really need to know. You see, it's the children and Barb's mother. Mr. Forrest doesn't believe me and if she takes the kids — "

"Calm down, Maris. Here, take another cup of tea. Plenty of sugar. You're overwrought."

"I'm not overwrought." Maris heard her voice getting higher. Like starting an argument with her mother, defending, defending. She took a deep breath. "I'm concerned, that's all. Mrs. Rice is planning to kidnap the kids."

Mrs. Dunkley gave a small snort. "Oh, surely not."

"If you can believe people turn into wolves, why can't you believe in a simple thing like kidnapping?"

"But she's their grandmother. It isn't kidnapping."

"Sure it is. Derek . . . Mr. Forrest . . . doesn't want them to go. But she's going to take them to America anyway."

Mrs. Dunkley put her cup down and folded her hands.

"I heard her talking about it to a lawyer on the phone," Maris said.

"Yes, yes. This is very bad news indeed."

Maris suddenly felt light-headed. Someone actually believed her. She leaned back against the chair and let out a sigh of relief.

"This is no time to relax, dear girl! Under no circumstances must the children be separated from their father, and certainly not taken out of the country. Oh, my, when you said kidnapping, I thought you meant they were going to the seashore. I'm sorry I appeared incredulous."

"It's okay," Maris said. "Mr. Forrest didn't believe me, either."

Mrs. Dunkley looked shocked. "You mean to tell me he isn't concerned? Has he taken steps to prevent this?"

Maris leaned forward. "He doesn't take it seriously, Mrs. Dunkley. That's why I had to speak to you."

"Well, now I'm as worried as you are. This could be dangerous for everybody. Barbara was convinced the children were all right — they have no marks — but there's no certainty until they're older. It's best for them to stay here." She looked up again at Maris. "They tend to exploit people in America, don't they? Anyone who's a little different?"

Maris felt bewildered. "I don't understand. What's wrong with Adam and Vicky?"

"Nothing is *wrong*. But there are those who see it differently."

"Do you mean they could have inherited something from Barb?"

"You make it sound like a disease. It's a gift, you know."

Maris was incredulous. "You're not saying she could actually do it . . . what did you call it, shapeshift?" Maybe Barb had been one of those people who went into trances and tried to project their spirits. "Is that why she killed herself?"

Mrs. Dunkley became brisk. "Never mind that. The issue at hand is to prevent the children from being taken away from their father."

Maris had found an ally. Mrs. Dunkley could do what Maris couldn't. She could find out things about lawyers and immigration and passports. She had friends and connections in the social services bureau where she volunteered. She could ask questions and she would get answers.

Suddenly Maris was shaking. She had not realized how much of a strain all of this had been.

"Are you all right?"

"Yes. I'm fine now. I'm really fine. Mrs. Dunkley, I really appreciate your helping."

"Of course you do, my dear. But you must promise me one thing."

"Anything."

"Don't ask too many questions. Don't probe too deeply. It's best if we simply work to prevent Barbara's mother from taking the children. Let us concentrate on that."

In a way, Mrs. Dunkley reminded Maris of Mrs. Li. Something wise and knowing in her eyes. Assuring. "Yes, all right, but . . . does Mr. Forrest know?"

"Know what? You were the one who said he wasn't aware of Mrs. Rice's intentions."

"About shapeshifting . . . about Barb thinking she could do it? He didn't know about this society, did he?"

Mrs. Dunkley gave her a long look. "No more questions. Just action. I'll find out what I can and phone you."

Maris hesitated. "Don't call. Write to me. It's better that way."

She gave Mrs. Dunkley a hug and left to catch the bus to Kelton, and then on to Banfield. A burden had been lifted. Everything would be okay.

But on the bus, looking out the window and seeing normal people doing normal things, Maris felt uneasy. Suppose Mrs. Dunkley was crazy? Maybe nobody would pay attention to her inquiries? Maybe she would give Maris all kinds of wrong information.

Maris sat back and closed her eyes. If that were true, there was nothing else she could do. She had promised to protect Adam and Vicky, but it might not be possible. Which meant Dottie Rice would take them away and Maris would be sent home.

As if that wasn't depressing enough, an even blacker thought came to her: What if Mrs. Dunkley had told the truth? That was far worse than her being crazy. Because then there really might be something wrong with the children, and she'd have to tell Derek. He'd never believe her. How could anyone believe he had been married to a . . . werewolf?

CHAPTER TWENTY-TWO

She waited. The moonlight streamed in through the windows, turning the room into black and white even though a lamp was lit on the desk.

He finished reading the papers she had given him and looked up.

"Now do you believe me?"

He sighed. Pushed the papers away across the desk. "Yes, Maris. I believe you."

Silence. Didn't he have more to say? Coldness leaked from him, crept across the room, and touched Maris in her heart.

"Well, aren't you even going to thank me?" Her voice had an edge, that high defensive tone.

"Thank you."

She tried to contain the anger she felt. The silence continued. He just sat there, looking at her with his gray-brown eyes. His fingers began to tap on the edge of the desk, but he still seemed calm, a frozen kind of calm. She looked at his fingers. The same length. All his fingers were the same length.

"Is that all you're going to say?"

"I do appreciate what you've done, Maris. I had no idea Dottie would go so far."

"So what will you do?"

"Stop her. I never intended letting her take the children."

"Oh, well, excuse me, I shouldn't have bothered."

"Look, there's no need for all of this."

The anger had to come out. He should be thanking her, telling her she did a good job. She'd gone to all that effort and he was acting as if it were nothing. "No need for what? I kept telling you what she was doing and you ignored me. You were so complacent, like you had everything under control. But you didn't really know all this was going on and you didn't even know about your own wife!"

He straightened in his chair. "What about Barbara?"

"What she was involved in. I told you, the society, they *believe* stuff like werewolves. Only they call it shapeshifting."

He made a dismissive gesture. "The 'society.' I would have preferred you hadn't contacted those crackpots."

"Mrs. Dunkley isn't a crackpot. If I hadn't talked to her, you wouldn't have all that information in your hands right now."

"Yes, well, don't have any more to do with her or the society. They're dangerous."

The idea of Mrs. Dunkley being dangerous made Maris feel like laughing. "You're only saying that because you don't want to know the truth about Barb."

"There's nothing I want to hear from that group. Barbara was a good person, a good mother."

He was glorifying her, just like Dottie Rice always did.

"What if I told you . . ." Maris began. She took a deep breath. "What if I told you Barb believed she was one of those shapeshifters?"

"What an absurd idea."

"Mrs. Dunkley said Barb was afraid the children might be the same way."

"Barbara was ill."

Maris laughed. "I'll say! She thought she was a werewolf."

She stopped laughing when she saw the expression on his face. She hadn't meant to say all this, the way she said it. She had only meant to convince him about Mrs. Rice so she wouldn't take the kids.

He was staring at her, through her, half smiling. She felt afraid.

"You're getting into deep water, Maris. Are you sure you can swim on?"

"I just meant that maybe Barb wasn't the saint you and her mother think she was." It was lame, but she didn't know what else to say to take it back.

"No, she wasn't a saint. Who is? But she wasn't a shapeshifter, as you call it, either."

"Okay. Okay." This was getting too crazy. What had happened? How had her good intentions turned into this stupid argument about werewolves?

"She tried very hard," Derek said quietly, almost meditatively. "But she could never manage a complete transition." He fixed his eyes on Maris. "Quite frankly, the whole idea revolted her."

"What?"

"She could never manage to shift her shape."

Maris felt her mouth open with surprise. She clamped it shut and abruptly sat down, even more surprised that her knees had turned into jelly. "I don't understand."

"That's right. You don't understand. You've jumped to all the wrong conclusions because you wanted to stay here in England."

Fear made her cold. Her jelly knees began to shake. She put her hands on them. "No, I didn't. . . ."

"It is the truth, isn't it? You want to stay here and the only way you can do that is to make sure the children also stay."

Maris felt the familiar fire and ice of humiliation prickle her scalp: every time her mother had found her out, every time she had a secret and her mother knew, every time she had been pleased and her mother ruined the pleasure. It was like having someone inside your brain, knowing everything, your most intimate, hidden thoughts.

"Why are you doing this to me?" she said miserably.

"Why are *you* doing this to *me*?" he asked back.

Maris looked down, suddenly ashamed. "I thought I was helping. I wanted to be right, for a change. I don't want to go home. I hate it there. I wish I never had to go back."

"What if you didn't have to?"

"Don't make fun of me."

"It's a serious question."

"How could I not go back? I mean . . . school . . ." She didn't like being teased. She didn't want to hear fantasies that would never come true. "Look, I know I screwed up. But I'm not stupid. It's a nice idea, but it could never happen."

"What if I could make it happen?"

She felt like crying. "How?"

"If you really want something, you must be willing

to go after it. If you want a change, you must make one yourself."

"Come on!" Maris cried. "I know all about positive attitudes and changing yourself. But I can't become somebody else's daughter. My mother is going to stay my mother."

"We were talking about a different kind of change before. Shifting a shape."

"Stop doing this," Maris said, feeling tired and empty and almost not caring what happened anymore. "Big change for you," Mrs. Li had warned. Maybe the big change was simply defeat. She had tried and it hadn't worked and now all she could do was go back home.

But even as she thought this, she was fighting it. Derek was speaking and she felt she had to get away so she could sort out her thoughts. She didn't want him to confuse her; she didn't want to listen. But she heard anyway.

"It's me. I'm the shapeshifter. I'm the wolf."

She didn't answer. She stood at the door, feeling his eyes boring into her back.

"You don't like that, do you?"

A tremor in her heart threatened to erupt all over her body.

"You liked it better when you thought it was Barbara."

That was true. The strangeness of it had seemed all right when it was her.

"You do realize that it will be hard for you to return home after this?"

"Why?" She turned to face him. "What do you mean?" she asked warily.

"You said you wanted to help me." His mouth looked cruel, his eyes stony, his face cold as iron. "Did you mean that?"

She nodded.

Then his face softened and looked lonely, and he glanced away. "There's really only one way you can help me. And I really have no right to ask you."

"I'll do it," she heard herself saying in spite of wanting to run from the room. A vision of herself at the airport, dragged along by Dottie Rice, seemed salvation.

"Don't agree to something before you know what it is!"

"But if it's more information . . . if . . ."

"No more information, no papers, none of that!" Roughly, he pushed the papers aside and they dropped to the floor. "Helping me means giving up everything. There's no way back, no way out, no way to undo it. Once it happens, it lasts forever." He laughed at her, standing there with her back to the door. "You can't imagine that, can you? All your bravado, all your melodrama. You don't know what to do with reality."

Anger energized her and the helplessness that had

always swamped her in an argument faded away. She felt she could be stronger, could say things he would listen to. "Tell me reality, then," she said. "Stop talking in riddles."

"The word means what it says: shapeshifting. Shifting the shape of man into the shape of a wolf. Becoming the wolf. Becoming all parts of the wolf, in mind, in body, in soul."

"A wolf . . . hunts. Kills things."

"It eats flesh."

She wanted to say, *This is all a joke, right?* But then she remembered the ruptured flesh of Barb's wrists, the jagged edges of bloodied skin, the bluish veins, like twists of broken thread. She choked her saliva back. What was it like to drink blood?

He looked forlorn, someone impossibly alone with himself. He really believed he could turn into a wolf and he wanted her to believe it, just as he had wanted Barb to believe. Maybe he really could arrange for her to stay here. But was he dangerous, or just crazy?

Time had ticked by as Maris thought. He had not moved from the desk or said a word. But now he leaned back and stretched, and the mood of the room changed.

"I had a feeling about you, Maris." He shrugged. "Just wishful thinking. Never mind."

"You're brushing me off."

He twisted his long fingers together and looked

thoughtful. "You know, Dottie is right. I am responsible for Barb's death, just as if I'd killed her with my own hands. She knew everything about me before our marriage and wanted to share it. I think, like you, she thought it was incidental, a little blip in my sanity that could be cured."

Maris blushed. Before she could answer, he went on, his voice sad. "She couldn't handle it, no matter how hard she tried. She insisted on going out with me, but it made her sick every time. I shouldn't have asked her. I should have kept my secret." He looked up and smiled.

Maris pushed her fear away. She wouldn't allow herself to think of Barb ripping out her veins in an attempt to show Derek she could be a wolf. Both of them, Derek and Maris, had gone too far. Something inside told her that now she had to stay. That if she tried to leave, he would stop her.

"I want to help."

"It's not pretend, Maris. It's real. Do you have the courage to find out how real?"

She took a deep breath. Go slow, she told herself. But her heart was thundering *yes yes yes*.

"You have to understand," she began, sounding like her own mother. "This is hard for me. It seems unreal right now. But I'm willing to try." She looked him in the eye. "You always scared me."

He frowned. "I never meant to frighten you. I worried about you. That time you went out and didn't return on the bus. I went to find out."

"Barb told me. But I never saw your car."

"I was there, following you. You were never out of my sight. Nothing could have harmed you while I was watching."

Marvis shivered. That shape, ghostly white, tracking her steps in the dark.

"But I was frightened. You must have seen I was scared! How could you just stand there watching?"

"I was in my other self. I acted the way that self must act. I know you feel afraid now; it's natural. But it won't always be so. Now, I've told you my secret. Will you give me something in return?"

He got up from the desk.

"What?" she asked, unable to stop herself from shrinking back against the door.

"It's nothing you can't give easily," he said as he walked toward her. "An embrace. Nothing more."

She took a tentative step to meet him. He put out his arms and enfolded her.

She felt herself going down down down, through her skin and into her bones, into the inside of her bones, walking through the marrow of her existence. Outside was the boiling of her blood. Inside was silence. Inside, somewhere, was the meaning of everything if only she could find it.

Father. Mother. I have never belonged to you. I have

waited a long time for some kind of belonging. I have always hoped to belong to someone.

She felt as if she were giving herself up, breath by breath, moving into sanctuary. She didn't want to examine this sanctuary too closely. She was aware of a tearing in her heart, a rending cry in his, as if they had exchanged souls for a moment. Now that she was so close to him, she wasn't sure she liked it. The idea of things could often be easier than living the reality.

Is this supposed to feel like love? she asked herself.

"This is your life in my life," he replied, as if she had spoken aloud. He did nothing more than hold her, caress her hair, keep her against him.

She felt everything draining out of her, all of her past, all of what she was. She had no more will of her own; she would do whatever he asked her to do. She was slipping into some kind of muted state, a quiet dream. She was tired. Sleepy.

"What should I do?" she asked.

"Nothing," he said.

She could feel his heart beating in his chest. Its rhythm was disturbing. She was frightened as her own heart struggled to match the beat of his. She didn't like the feeling it gave her, of something untamed and ferocious.

CHAPTER TWENTY-THREE

Her dreams were full of dark images, creatures half human, half animal, growling at her, baring teeth. She kept waking up, her heart going like a bedspring. What if he had been playing an elaborate joke? What if he was insane? Would she go as mad as Barb?

The morning sunshine didn't help. She woke too early, groaned, and closed her eyes again. She had felt like this once before, after her father left. Bad dreams then, too, awakening in the morning with a split second's worth of calm before the knowledge hit her. Calm replaced by a sense of unreality, of watching herself on film, knowing there was no going back to the way it had been before.

She dragged herself down to the kitchen. Adam and

Vicky were at the table, slopping cereal around in their bowls. Dottie was drinking decaffeinated coffee.

"I had an idea," she said. She wanted to take the kids to Kelton to buy clothes. "They'll need them for school this fall. No sense relying on their father. He doesn't have a clue what to get them."

"Did Derek . . . Mr. Forrest say it was okay?"

Dottie gave her a look. "Do I need permission? Of course he said yes. He's grateful that I'm here to help him take care of the children."

"That's what I'm here for," Maris said.

"Yes, well, today I'll take charge and you can do the few things Agnes would have done. She won't be coming every day anymore." She got up from the table and took her cup to the sink. "I'll just get the keys to Barb's car and we'll be off."

Adam looked worried. "You said we shouldn't let her take us anywhere in the car," he whispered to Maris.

"It's all right," she told him. "She's only taking you shopping."

But she followed Dottie into the sitting room to check that her luggage was still piled up in the corner behind the sofa, and that her stuff was scattered around.

Yet as Maris watched the car disappear down the lane, she was stricken with panic. The business about school clothes was nonsense. The clothes would be for a trip to America. What if Dottie had been more than clever, leaving all her luggage behind on purpose? She could be taking the kids to the airport right now.

She felt helpless. Why wasn't Derek here to tell her what to do? His office number was written on the emergency list tacked up in the kitchen, but she felt awkward about phoning him. Would he call her melodramatic again?

Maris's mouth felt dry. She turned on the kitchen tap and got a glass of water, then let the water flow over her hands and wrists, almost a kind of cleansing. She sat down on one of the kitchen chairs and tried to force herself to relax.

The phone shrieked and she jumped.

"Maris, are you alone?"

"Oh. Derek. I'm so glad you called. Dottie took the children to Kelton to buy them clothes. I — "

"How long ago did they leave?"

"Just now, but I'm worried — "

"Stop worrying. Promise?"

"I'll try."

"Stay inside the house. Wait for me."

She replaced the receiver. She looked out into the garden. The sun glinted through the trees, opening and closing like an eye. He had been out there once. Watching her, smiling at her.

Wait for me.

Suddenly she knew. She sat down again in the

kitchen chair. Her body tingled. She forced herself to breathe deeply. Slowly, her heartbeat calmed. There was no escaping this. No using her mother's excuses — "I don't feel well, I think I'm getting a sore throat" — no backing down. She'd made a decision. She would accept whatever happened. There was no turning back anyway. How could she give up, go home to everything she had wanted to escape?

"Let it happen," she whispered. "I'm ready for whatever it is."

Only, somewhere deep in her heart, she hoped she wouldn't die.

There was a noise at the garden door. A gentle scratching. A quiet breathing.

Her body went rigid with cold fear in spite of her determination; her heart threatened to begin pounding again. Flight or fright, the instinctive reaction, hard to quell. She forced herself to stay seated. But she kept her eyes away from the door. She didn't want to see it yet.

An animal was in the room with her. All of her senses were acutely aware of its presence. She could feel it, smell it, taste it. Her mind's eye could even see it. Slowly she turned her head.

Before her was a great white wolf. The shape was familiar, but so incongruous in the setting that it seemed larger, more potent, more dangerous than it would have in a forest. The flight reaction charged through her so powerfully that Maris could feel her feet moving under her and it was all she could do to keep from running away. She made herself look at him without flinching.

His shape was different, but his eyes were the same. He had told her: *Don't be afraid. I will never harm you.*

He could not speak to her in words now, only whine in his throat and mewl softly as he stood in the doorway, imploring her not to panic. She nodded. A warmth began to spread over her. She no longer wanted to run. She was ready for him.

He came toward her. She could feel his hot breath before his black muzzle actually touched her knees. He waited, as if asking her permission, and again she nodded. His head moved onto her legs. She felt the weight of it, the heat of it. Hesitantly, she touched the very tips of his ears. Suddenly he pushed forward, nuzzling the soft flesh at the inside of her knee.

She shivered and he hesitated. But her shivering was not out of fear. She let her hand move toward his neck.

The bite, stinging but tender, drew blood. He licked it away, watching her eyes. *Maris, I will never harm you.*

In one long shuddering tremor, she knew she had been blooded. She put her own fingers into the blood on her knee, lifted them, and smeared her cheeks.

And then Dottie screamed.

"Oh, my God, a rabid dog! Children, children, run quick."

Dottie reached blindly at the sink, picked up a saucepan, swung it madly as she approached them.

"Get away, get away, shoo," she said. "Maris run, run."

She swung the pot at his head, but the wolf was too quick for her.

"For God's sake, get up, Maris!" Dottie yelled.

Maris moved dreamily, following Derek to the doorway. She knelt down and put her arms around the thick ruff of his white neck and kissed him.

This is the love I have never felt. All I want to do is hold you like this, warmth of my heart.

Dottie was on top of them. A blow from the pot glanced off the wolf's head, hit Maris in the cheek. With her other hand, Dottie pounded blindly at Maris with her fist. "Stupid, stupid, get away from it!" she screamed.

The wolf bared its teeth. Its fur bristled. It moved back slightly, stiffening its haunches, ready to pounce.

A low agonized whine came from its throat. Its head thrashed, as if fighting indecision. With one long howl, Derek was standing there, naked, Maris still at his feet, hugging his knees. His hands were in her hair, yanking at the roots, as he struggled between his two selves.

Dottie screamed and her eyes rolled up into her head. Her white-knuckled hand went limp and the pot clanged to the floor. Dottie fell after it, as if she were dissolving, first her ankles giving way, then her knees. She let out a long, shuddering sigh.

Derek knelt over her, feeling for a pulse in her neck. "She's dead."

Maris stared, hardly able to believe that it happened so fast. Could a person just die of fright like that? "Her heart . . . ?"

"Call Dr. Spears while I get dressed."

Maris nodded, but she didn't move. "Why did she come back? They were supposed to be shopping for clothes. The children! What if they saw you?"

He shook his head. "They ran into the woods. They only saw a dog."

Adam and Vicky didn't ask many questions. They had been on the road to Kelton when Dottie realized she had forgotten her credit cards and had turned back. They accepted that the big dog had gone away, that their grandmother had died. It wasn't normal, their acceptance. When Maris looked into their strangely tearless eyes, she saw something there; not suspicion or fear, but knowledge.

"It's in their blood, too," Derek told her. "But they don't understand it all yet."

Dr. Spears asked no awkward questions, either. It was obvious that Mrs. Rice had had a massive heart attack. She had been on medication for years. Stress, he said. Too much stress over the death of her daughter. "Crying shame, really," he said as he snapped his bag shut. "Don't worry about the police," he said to Derek. "I'll file the death certificate. There won't be trouble."

Maris thought, Was the doctor a member of the society, protecting the wolves? Or maybe the doctor was a shapeshifter himself. There might be more of them out there. How would Maris ever know who was and who wasn't?

PART THREE

CHAPTER TWENTY-FOUR

There were times when it all seemed like a dream. Waking in the early morning, when pale light first seeped into the bedroom, she thought she must have imagined the wolf, that she had been given a drug, that Dottie Rice was still alive and on Friday they would be going back to America.

No. Dottie Rice was dead and Maris was changed. There was a strange new taste in her saliva. Her teeth ached. Sometimes, when she saw MacDuff's cage, she felt drawn to it. She quickly turned away, not wanting to see the small warm body huddled in the straw.

The children had taken their grandmother's death in a quiet, solemn way. Maris wondered if they were suffering from some kind of delayed shock. Two deaths in such a short time. But of course they had not really loved Mrs. Rice. There was no knowing who they loved.

Who did Maris love? She watched Derek for signs of a change in his feelings toward her. She saw little. He seemed to expect her to go on doing what she had always done: look after the children, help with the meals. Except that she was taking on more of the burden. After Mrs. Rice's death, Agnes had refused to come back. She gave her arthritis as the reason, but Maris wondered if Agnes was afraid, or thought the house was bad luck. If Derek noticed how hard Maris worked, he never mentioned it. And Maris was afraid to ask about another cleaner. She felt she was on tenterhooks, waiting for something to happen; and whatever it was, it was secret, forbidden. Better Agnes wasn't around. Maris found meat in the freezer and staples in the larder and did her best. Sometimes Adam or Vicky gave advice.

"You're supposed to use yellow cheese for macaroni cheese," Adam said.

"There is no yellow cheese," Maris said. "And anyway, this is not macaroni and cheese. It's pasta with ham and tomatoes."

"It looks like spaghetti," Vicky said. "Only the spaghetti is supposed to be long and stringy."

"There is no spaghetti, either," Maris said.

They ate what she served without too much complaining. Maris sometimes looked at her plate, after she had served herself whatever mishmash she had cooked, and felt sick to her stomach. Her jaw ached. Her teeth hurt. She tasted lead in her mouth.

Derek had not gone out in the night, nor had he taken her out. He had told her, after Dr. Spears had gone and Mrs. Rice's body had been taken away, that he would initiate her, that he would show her his private world of night. But he had done nothing.

"When will it be?" she had asked him. She wasn't sure if she was happy about it, but it was a longing inside her, something unfulfilled, something she needed to know. How would it feel to change? Would it hurt? What if she couldn't change herself back?

"Do we have to wait for a full moon or something?" she joked, trying to tease him into a promise.

He laughed harshly. "Your head is full of old wives' tales. Wolves hunt when they need food; they are not subject to the whims of the moon."

"How will I know when I need food?" she asked, thinking of the sickening dinners, thinking of the taste in her mouth.

"You may not like it at first. You may never like it. There's every possibility of your reacting exactly as Barbara did: repulsed, revolted."

"I'm different. I want to do it."

"Barbara wanted to do it, too."

She felt a pang of jealousy. "Did . . . could she change her shape?"

"She couldn't give herself up to it completely. But she went with me regardless, to protect me, she said, even forced herself to eat the kill. She did it because she loved me, but it always made her sick. She was a stubborn woman in her own way."

"She once said she loved you too much."

"Perhaps that's what cost her her life."

"I won't be like that," Maris said.

"You don't know yet."

"You'll see," she said.

She forced herself to be patient. But the waiting grew tedious and then boring, and then suddenly imperative.

Her mother phoned one afternoon. Of course it was early morning in the States. Adam happened to be near the telephone and he answered it and said, unprompted, that Maris wasn't at home.

"She said to ring her back," Adam reported to Maris, who had been sitting at the kitchen table, flipping through the pages of a recipe book. "She said it didn't matter what the time was because she had something important to tell you."

Maris didn't do anything. She made no decision about it, she simply let the hours drift into the evening and then a day. When the phone rang the next morning, she ignored it. When it rang in the middle of the night, she bolted up and waited, holding her breath in the hall, to see if Derek would get up, but the ringing went on, and finally stopped.

Soon after, a man in a uniform, pushing a bicycle, came up the lane to the house. It gave Maris a shock. She had seen no one outside the family since the ambulance had come for Mrs. Rice. The uniform frightened her until she realized it wasn't the police or someone else who could force her to go back to America. When he handed her the telegram, she almost gave it back. She wondered whether she should tip him. She stood on the doorstep, dithering until he went away.

She didn't want to read the telegram. She placed it in the middle of the kitchen table and let it stay there all afternoon, driving Vicky and Adam crazy with curiosity.

"What if it's a surprise?" Vicky asked.

"What if it's bad news?" asked Adam.

"I know what it is," Maris said.

Just before Derek was due home, she ripped through the seal with trembling fingers. She stared at the words, alternately feeling joy and despair.

RETURN HOME IMMEDIATELY. CONTACT MR. REYNOLDS, U.S. EMBASSY, LONDON, OR HE WILL CONTACT YOU. MOTHER

Adam and Vicky waited, wide-eyed.

"You're both right," Maris told them. "It's a bad-news surprise."

"What can the American Embassy do to me?" she asked Derek when he arrived home.

She handed him the telegram. "Can they deport me or something?"

"I don't see how. Your six-month visa is in order. You told them you planned to stay until the end of the summer. Surely they can't be bothered about a domestic dispute between a mother and teenager."

The word hit Maris like a blow. Teenager! "If that's what you think of me . . ." She turned to leave the room, tears stinging her eyes.

He grabbed her arm. "Maris, don't be silly. I didn't think, I'm sorry."

"You're just playing games with me," she said.

"No. Never games."

When the time came, there was no warning or special preparation. She didn't know until he came home and told her to make sure the children got to bed early. He instructed her to give them hot cocoa before they went upstairs.

"Read them a story until they get drowsy," he said.

"But what if they wake up while we're out?"

He indicated the mugs of cocoa with a nod. "That will ensure they won't wake up until morning."

"What have you put in there?"

"Nothing dangerous. Trust me." He looked at her. "The alternative is that we don't go."

She was torn. It wasn't right to drug the kids, but her heart was hammering with anticipation. He was their father. It would be all right, wouldn't it? This might be her only chance. Every day she was scared that Mr. Reynolds would appear from London and do something to make her leave.

"All right," she said, and gave the cocoa to the children.

They drove through the country lanes, about five miles from the house. Derek parked in a copse, a place he had used before.

"Take off your clothes," he said.

"Why?"

"Wolves don't wear clothes. We need to take them off beforehand."

Maris thought of the werewolf movies, in which clothing magically and conveniently disappeared and reappeared.

Hesitantly, she began to undress, turned away from Derek, suddenly embarrassed. Suppose this was all a ruse? How stupid it would be, to explain that she willingly undressed before she was attacked.

Yes, stupid, Maris, she thought. You saw the wolf. You saw him change, right in front of your eyes, in front of Dottie's eyes. This is not a joke.

They stood naked together in the moonlight. This, she thought, has nothing to do with jokes. It may have everything to do with love. I am doing this because of him. Why would I do this unless I love him? Do I love him or is this something else, an answer to an old longing, something I've known inside me, that had always been there? Destiny, Mrs. Li once said, happens whether you want it or not.

Derek's eyes went black, opaque, silver. He seemed to suck himself inward. His body glowed, radiated an aura; the aura exploded like a supernova, receded, shimmered white, melted. He was there again in front of her: the white wolf.

Come, Maris, he said without words. And then he was gone. She ran after him, desperate to catch up, until her muscles burned, her breath came in ragged bursts. There were moments when she imagined she was like him, a beautiful animal racing to the hunt. But she was always aware that she ran on two feet, in her human body. She had new strength, but she was still Maris. She wondered, if she failed to change, would he kill her?

They came out of the woods into a pasture full of the huddled shapes of sheep, like woolen haystacks. The sheep stirred only slightly. The white wolf lowered its great white head and stealthily moved forward. A ripple went through the herd, but they settled again. And then, all at once they were awake and in blind panic, milling around and bleating. They broke into a disorganized run. Deftly, the white wolf cut out the weakest ewe. His fangs glittered as he jumped at her neck. His sharp teeth cracked bone, crunched muscle, and gristle, brought the ewe down.

He raised his head and looked at Maris. Another part of the blooding. It was her turn to feel raw death in her mouth. To eat.

She hesitated, remembering her promise not to be like Barb. Her jaw ached, her teeth gnashed, saliva dripped from her mouth. And yet she was still human. A naked girl standing in a pasture, the night air cool on her pale skin, trying to cover herself with her hands, while next to her the animal watched, fur bristling, fangs dripping. Don't hold back. Give in, give in. *Oh, help me*, she prayed to no god in particular, and the prayer became a harsh sound, rasping out of her throat.

The white wolf licked blood from the ewe's neck and offered his tongue to her. She inched forward, crouching, suddenly down on all fours, her hands digging into the soil. Neck stretched forward, she crawled to him, offered him her lips. Delicately, slowly, she tasted the blood, salt sour, its piquancy unfamiliar for only a moment.

And then the shape of her bones began to shift, and she could feel the change in her, like a fire turned on deep in her loins, churning into full flame, spreading and crackling as flesh and cartilage gave way to new form, as sharp angles replaced soft curves, as her body became a fierce instrument of the night, a finely tuned hunting machine. For a moment her face seemed broken as fangs cut into her lips before they drew back in a lupine smile. The molten fire reached her throat. She coughed and growled.

My humanness has scampered away like a frightened toad. This knowledge of who I now am plows me, deepens me, pushes me through time. I know everything. I know where fox and deer have walked, where turtle crawled, where badger crept. Delectation. I know the happiness of the hunt, the honor of the pack, and I know the sadness and pain of our annihilation.

Her mouth was at the ewe's neck. She heard a snarl as she put her teeth to the flesh. The taste was wet, raw, smoky. For a moment she felt she could not continue. Her insides threatened to erupt. She fought the bitterness of her bile, the feeling of this repulsive death in her mouth.

I am not human. I am a wolf. I am my other self. I will do as my other self commands.

She forced herself to chew. To swallow.

Didn't I tell you, Derek, that I was different?

CHAPTER TWENTY-FIVE

Maris was relieved to see that Adam and Vicky woke up normally and showed no aftereffects of the drug. She had worried about it, in the hour before dawn, after she and Derek had wearily driven home and she crawled into bed. Maris was surprised that Derek simply went to his room and closed the door in her face. She had stood in the dark hallway a moment, wondering. But she was overcome by tiredness, and the romantic ideas that had churned in her brain earlier were dulled. Her exultant energy spent, she was left with cramps in her limbs and a foul taste in her mouth. She went into the bathroom, willing herself not to vomit, and bathed and used mouthwash.

Yet once in bed, sleep did not come and she began to worry about the children, feeling guilty for what she had let Derek do. It didn't help to tell herself that he was their father. She had come to England to prove she could be responsible. It was not responsible to leave Adam and Vicky alone in the house, no matter how safe Derek said it was.

Maris had expected, after the blooding, that Derek would act differently toward her. Sitting at the kitchen table the next morning, the memory of the hunt flared in her mind. She looked across at him, half expecting some palpable fire to flash between them. But Derek drank his coffee and talked to the children as if it were just another ordinary day. Maris could see nothing in his actions, in his eyes, that showed he even remembered.

It left her hurt. Small at first, she picked at the hurt feeling throughout the day, her mind only half on what she was doing until it was a swollen, aggravated sore by the time Derek returned home.

But she kept herself in check, waiting to see if there was any change in him. Excitement began to tingle inside her, too, as she wondered if they would go out again that night.

She botched the dinner, trying to impress him with American fried chicken. The chicken tasted nothing like it should have; she didn't know how to fry chicken anyway. There was raw flesh and dark blood around the bones, where the meat had not defrosted properly. Maris noticed that Derek didn't seem to mind. He ate greedily and sucked at the bones. She had no appetite. She pushed the food around on her plate indifferently. And yet she had felt hungry when she was cooking. Now the food looked about as appetizing as cardboard.

"Not hungry, Maris?" Derek asked.

"Not really."

"I'm not hungry, either," Adam said, shoving his plate aside.

"Me either," said Vicky.

"You two eat your dinners," Derek said sternly.

Maris sympathized when they made faces, but something in Derek's attitude kept her from speaking. She pretended she agreed with him and hoped there would not be a scene.

When he was finished, Derek got up from the table and went into the sitting room. In a few moments, the sounds of a television program drifted out. Maris surveyed the messy table.

"Come on, let's clean up," she said.

Adam and Vicky obediently brought their plates to the sink and began collecting the rest.

Maris ran hot water into the basin and began scrubbing the dirty dishes. In the sitting room, Derek laughed at something funny on television. Maris's hands grew red in the soapy water. What is this? she thought. A voice deep within her replied: *What you wished for.*

Vicky danced around the kitchen floor with a dish towel on her head. Adam egged her on.

"Cut it out," Maris snapped. "You're supposed to be helping."

She left the fryer full of greasy oil in the sink and went to find Derek.

"I might as well just be some stupid au pair girl!" she shouted at him.

"You are not stupid, Maris. But you are the au pair."

"How can you do this to me?"

"Do what to you?"

"Treat me this way. When will you take me out again? When can we hunt again?"

He looked around. "Be careful how you talk."

She lowered her voice. "Well, when?"

"Not right away. This isn't some game."

"I never thought it was a game!"

She turned to leave the room, but he called her back. "Look, Maris, I'm sorry there's this misunderstanding. But . . . I don't know how to explain it to you. This isn't something I do all the time. There are times, in fact, when I would prefer not to do it at all. You're young and you think — "

"I thought you would be glad. Not lonely anymore. I thought it was what you wanted."

He looked away. "Yes, but I also regret it. My life hasn't been happy this way. I was selfish about Barb and now I'm being selfish about you."

"But I wanted to." She touched his arm. "It must have been there in me all along, otherwise how could I have changed? Barb tried and she couldn't. I'm different. I know it inside. Somehow, you must have known it, too." Her face grew hot as she remembered his teeth on her flesh, marking her with the wound that still had not healed. The intimacy of that act . . . doing it to Barb. Now her.

"It's all right, Maris," he said more gently. "But have patience. You're too eager to have it all right now. Leave it alone for a while. There's plenty of time for the future to unfold."

But Maris could not wait for a future that might never come. She could not ignore Mr. Reynolds and the American Embassy. And even if, by some miracle, she managed to stay for the six-month visa stamped on her passport, what would happen after that?

She felt herself on the brink of tears.

"This is all too much for you to cope with alone," Derek was saying. "I'll phone Agnes and ask her to come back. If it's a matter of money, I'll increase her wage."

"Oh, no!" Maris said without thinking. "She doesn't like me," she added quickly.

"That's just her way; don't let it worry you."

"You always say don't worry. I'm afraid if she's here. I mean, about us. About going out at night."

"She'll only be here in the daytime, Maris. Stop this now and go see about getting the children to bed."

"But . . ."

"Yes?"

"Nothing."

What do you want with me? What will you do with me? Questions she couldn't ask him right now. Questions she might not like the answers to.

Did they look at her differently when she kissed them good night? Was Adam's long look an appraisal? Imagination, Maris told herself. Guilty conscience? The kids would know nothing; they had been in a drugged sleep.

Lying in bed, overcome by a strange longing, Maris thought of the forest, of how Derek had been different there: loving, tender, protective. *I will never harm you*, he had said. But words could harm. In the forest, there were no words.

She wanted to go back to the night, be part of it, the hunt, the feel of it in her limbs, in her teeth, on her tongue, that salt-sour-sweet taste of flesh and blood. No food could stop the yearning, although she poured salt into her hand and licked it up hungrily. She thought about eating raw steak, sucking at the cold blood. What was happening to her?

In the night she got up and stood at the window. I need to kill, she thought, and thought of MacDuff. She pushed the idea away. It came back. She felt a pulling deep inside her. No, she told herself. No, no. She walked backward to the bed. No.

There was a strange whining sound in the room. Frightened, she looked around. Who is it? Who's there? Derek?

But the sound was coming from her. And when she reached up to feel her face, she touched the wetness around her mouth. Her hand came back with blood on it. Cut by her own teeth. Razor sharp. She tried to hold on to her mind, to keep her thoughts focused. But black wind came in. It sang to her: *I want. I need.*

She could not stop herself.

CHAPTER TWENTY-SIX

How strange that one moment can be tentative and the next determined. She crept down the staircase, careful to step where it would creak the least. Derek's door was shut tight. She didn't care. All she wanted was to get out into the night. She opened and closed the kitchen door carefully. Then stopped to breath deeply.

Night forest, this is where I belong, your dark shadow child moving through the spaces between trees, knowing your every scent, dear forest, wet earth, mother of my wild heart.

Although she was still herself, she could feel the change coming. Her body curved, her senses sharpened, the dark in front of her eyes cleared. She was aware of every sound, the breathing of the fox, the shiver of the vole, the twitch of the owl. Stealthily, she made her way to the rabbit hutch and looked in.

The rabbit had flattened itself against the back wall of the cage. It was shaking and faintly whimpering.

"MacDuff, it's me."

Her voice was low and hoarse. She drew up. I can't do this, she thought. I love Adam and Vicky.

But neither could she return to her room and sleep. She looked beyond the garden. It would be easy to go into the woods, to undress, to run a little while.

She walked the length of the garden and entered the woods. Still in view of the house, in the faint golden glimmer of the garden lamp, she undressed and laid her clothes neatly on the ground.

Just for a few minutes, she told herself. A short run. A small hunt. I will do it myself this time. A tiny creature who will not make much noise.

Gristlecrunch, bonecrack, a new shape moved under her skin, shattering her flesh, cutting her into tiny slivers, pulling her inside out, pressing her down toward the earth, slavering her tongue against newly sharpened teeth.

She raced away. Freedom. Glorious scent of blood. She moved quickly, more graceful than she had been before, swifter, keener. A small stoat, clothed in its summer coat of brown, scampered before her. Effortlessly, she sprang. It was clenched between her jaws. She shook it violently, teeth clamping down into the flesh. Again that raw wet taste.

I will stop soon, she thought. But a stoat was a small meal. Somewhere, in the next corridor of darkness, would be something larger, more satisfying, a challenge to her skill.

She ran on, searching for game. Yet she was afraid to leave the enclosure of the woods, where she and Derek had once walked with the children, where he had sung, "Who's afraid of the big bad wolf?" It was an hour before she came back to herself. Only the unexpected scent of her own clothes reminded her the night would not last forever. She was back where she had started. The first watery light gave view to scudding clouds of dawn. In half an hour, the sky would turn pinkish blue.

There was a crackling in the wood and she turned sharply toward it but could not make out what it was. Her senses were suddenly dulled and confused. What was she? Who was she? As her strong animal's body gave way to its weak, human counterpart, she felt stinging pain, terrifying fear. She huddled naked and dirty, on cold ground, looking up at him.

"Maris, Maris," Derek said as he lifted her. She heard kindness in his voice. Or was it pity?

He carried her to the house, as tenderly and as effortlessly as he would a child. But once inside, he changed.

Forcing her to sit in a chair while he made tea, he began to scold.

"Nobody saw me," she said defensively.

"You cannot take the risk. You don't understand the danger."

"I stayed close by. I didn't leave the cottage woods."

"You won't be satisfied with this small private patch forever. As soon as you go farther out, you run the risk of getting shot. A farmer, a poacher, anybody who sees a wolf is going to either shoot it or report it. And there are traps, for other animals. How will you explain it when you're found naked in a trap?"

"You didn't seem worried about that the other night."

"Maris, I'm older than you. I've been doing this much longer. Believe me, there is not one moment of my life that is without danger."

"I never thought of you as being afraid."

"Only fools have no fear."

She was silent. She felt herself resisting his warning. He meant well. But she had been fearful too long. Now she had a way to make herself powerful and free. What could harm her when she could turn herself into a gray wolf and run like the wind?

"Think of the children if you can't think of yourself," he said. "How will you look after them if you stay up all night?"

Part of her rebelled at being reminded. Another part of her quaked in fear that he would hire someone to replace her, force her to go home.

"I'm sorry," she said in a chastened voice. "I didn't think. It's all so new to me."

"That's my girl. We'll work things out, you'll see. But no more of these escapades. Promise you'll be sensible from now on?"

She looked into his eyes. Nodded her head. Looked down into her tea and was suddenly revolted by the sight of the pale milky liquid floating in her cup like scum. It had been wonderful, out there in the forest. She would try to be sensible. But she couldn't promise it would never happen again. If the urgency of the night came back, and if he continued to refuse to go with her, she didn't know what she might do.

"Go get a couple of hours' sleep. I'll wake you before I go to the office."

She was so tired. Didn't have the strength to protest. If there was a next time, if she had to do it, she would be sensible. She would make sure he didn't find out.

CHAPTER TWENTY-SEVEN

Someone was forcing her awake. She didn't want to wake up. She wanted to sleep for a hundred years. A hand kept shaking her shoulder. A voice in her ear kept calling. "Maris, Maris, open your eyes."

"What time is it?" she asked, disoriented, wondering why she was so tired. Then it all came back and she felt a hole of breathless anxiety open up her chest.

"It's after nine. I have to go. The children are already downstairs."

She managed to croak. "Okay," but her heavy eyelids threatened to close again.

"Maris!"

"Sorry." She forced herself to get off the bed. Her

knees felt shaky. Her head ached, her ears buzzed. Her mouth felt as if it had been punched.

"Get some breakfast into you. Drink some coffee," Derek ordered.

Shyly, she put out her hand to touch his sleeve, but he drew his arm away. "I have to go now."

"Oh, all right!" She turned on her heel and stomped downstairs ahead of him.

Adam and Vicky stopped eating to survey her.

"Are you okay?" Adam asked.

"You look wonky," Vicky said.

"I'm fine. What are you two eating?" She took the chocolate biscuit box away from them. "It's too early for this junk."

"Mummy let us!" Vicky began to wail.

"Do as Maris tells you," Derek said from the doorway, and Vicky stopped.

When he had gone, a hollow feeling of loneliness gaped open inside her. The day stretched out before her, a long journey around the clock until six.

She thought of Mrs. Dunkley. Maybe she could invite her over. History repeats itself, she thought. That's what Barb did, asked old ladies to visit. But only they would understand. She could talk only to them. All of a sudden, she was seeing things through Barb's eyes. Without Derek, she wasn't only lonely, she was utterly alone.

There was a sound at the door and Maris thought, He's come back. But it was Agnes who came into the kitchen, already tying an apron around her waist. She looked at the table disapprovingly. Adam and Vicky slid out of their chairs and scuttled out of the room like two crabs going sideways.

"Breakfast over?" she asked archly, eyeing the clock.

"What are you doing here?"

"What I've been asked to do. I'll make myself a cup of tea, if you don't mind."

"Who asked you?"

Agnes harrumphed and snapped the electric kettle on. "Mr. Forrest rang me last night, didn't he?"

"Did he?" Perhaps he had. But what if her mother had somehow contacted Agnes? What if Agnes was there to make sure Mr. Reynolds could come and take her away? She slumped into one of the kitchen chairs. She was exhausted; her head ached and the bite on her knee, which had reopened last night, burned and throbbed. She couldn't imagine finding the energy to play with the children. All she wanted to do was sleep.

The phone rang. Agnes looked inquiringly at her and she looked back blank. She didn't want to answer the phone, but she didn't want Agnes to answer, either. Finally the ringing stopped and Adam's voice called from the hall, "It's Kerry for you, Maris."

He was asking if she wanted to go out with him.

If she hadn't been so tired, she might have laughed. Kerry, Brenda, dates . . . "No, Kerry, I don't think so."

"Look, I'm sorry about last time. It was a filthy joke."

"I really can't."

"So, another time? I'll give you a bell?"

"Maybe."

She put down the telephone. Agnes was hovering. "Was that your mother?"

"No, it was not my mother."

"She'll be worrying about you. And so she should be."

"I don't think it's any of your business."

"It isn't right, you know."

"What?"

"You staying in this house with him. A young girl and an older man."

"I'm employed here. Nothing else is going on."

"I didn't say there was. Yet."

Maris turned away. She didn't want to get into a fight. But the sea of loneliness sloshing around inside her began to rise. Angry tears sprang into her eyes.

"Why don't you just keep your suspicion to yourself!"

"Concern is what it is," Agnes said quietly. "No harm meant."

Disarmed by the woman's sudden gentleness, Maris

found herself saying awkwardly, "Okay. Forget it."

Agnes turned away and busied herself with a mop. "Concern is what decided me to come back here. I'd feel guilty if I kept my back turned. Just don't want to see it happen again."

"What happen?"

Agnes rubbed her hands on her apron. She looked torn between confiding in Maris and saying nothing. "Another death in this house," she said.

"Why should there be? Mrs. Rice had a bad heart and Barb . . . Barb was . . . disturbed."

"You don't know it all. House is named Sweet Poison. No good can come of that."

Maris felt a surge of fear and anger. She had to get away from Agnes. She went outside to Adam and Vicky, who were sitting in the grass. MacDuff, out of his cage, hopped between them. The sight stopped Maris in her tracks.

"He learned a new trick," Adam called to her.

"I . . . Maybe you better put him back," Maris said.

"He likes it out here with us," Vicky replied.

"I know, but . . ." But what? She might kill their pet in front of their eyes? She had to have more control than that. This was stupid. Derek didn't go around killing his children's pets. But then Maris thought about the lock on the rabbit's cage. The scream of an animal in the middle of the night. The fact that they had no dog. A dog hadn't liked

Derek. The dog down at Milestones had been killed.

"Put him back!" Maris ordered. They looked at her, startled.

"You're not afraid of MacDuff, are you?" Adam asked.

"Of course not!"

He and Vicky exchanged glances.

"Do rabbits and animals make you feel odd?" Vicky asked.

What were they driving at? "Not really. Maybe I'm allergic or something."

"Like Daddy," Vicky said. "Mummy wasn't allergic, though. She liked MacDuff."

"I like him, too," Maris said. "I just don't feel well."

They became solicitous. Adam locked MacDuff up; Vicky suggested she lie down on the grass and look up at the clouds. "Mummy used to do that sometimes."

Maris felt abashed. "Do you miss your mom a lot?"

They nodded.

Mixed emotions surged inside of Maris. Of course they missed their mother — they were just kids. They would go on missing her and Maris could never be more than second best, no matter how much they liked her. But then, had she really ever wanted to take Barb's place? She had wanted escape, from her mother, from the life back home, and this job in England had seemed just that.

But now another road to escape had opened up.

Some power she felt inside her but couldn't quite pin down. Could anyone or anything keep her now? If she could change herself, she could change her life. Except. Except she didn't know how. Not yet.

"Don't you miss your mum?" Adam asked.

Maris laughed. "Not much."

"A little?"

Maris thought about who she missed. Mrs. Li. Ms. Epstein. But she could live without them. Right now she missed the night. The dark. The hunt. She missed the thing she could not identify: long-ago atavistic memory that was now etched on her own soul. Again she found tears welling up in her eyes.

"What's the matter?" Adam asked, his childish voice cracking with concern.

"Maybe I am a little homesick."

"Will you have to go home someday?" Adam asked.

Maris was unable to answer. I don't know, she thought. I don't know where my home is anymore.

CHAPTER TWENTY-EIGHT

There were things happening in her body that she didn't understand. Eating had become a problem. At times she could hardly force herself to swallow a piece of toast. More often she gagged and her throat closed up. She lived on the tomato juice bought at the small Banfield grocery, an expensive elixir in a cardboard box. As she drank it greedily, she thought of its color, ruby red, and its texture, thick and creamy, like coagulated blood. When she looked into the mirror, she saw a thinner face, sharp cheekbones, dark hollows under her eyes. The skin was pale, almost sickly, but the eyes burned. She was afraid to smile into the mirror, afraid to see her teeth.

One night, Adam and Vicky asked her to defrost a lemon meringue pie. Maris served it, and took a piece for herself. She had not been able to eat dinner, but the pie suddenly looked appetizing. Afterward, she felt sick and ran to the bathroom. She threw up her pie, her body heaving long after there was nothing more inside. She was left with an aching in her throat, a hunger for what she could hardly admit to herself: newly killed raw flesh. Nothing else would satisfy her. She needed Derek to explain these things to her, to tell her whether it would get worse or better. He didn't eat much but had no trouble finishing a meal. He seemed to live an outwardly normal life, going to his office, reading newspapers, sleeping in his bed at night. Why was she so tormented when he wasn't?

She had tried. They had gone to the park at Banfield Rise for a picnic one day. The sky was a perfect robin's-egg blue, touched only by the wispiest of clouds. Shouts of children and the barking of dogs came through the trees. Everything was in full midsummer bloom. But to Maris, it was all happening behind a thick glass wall. She could not touch it or enjoy it. She could not shake herself back to normal. When the children scampered off to explore, she asked Derek.

"Why does nothing satisfy me except the thought of raw flesh and warm blood?"

"Come on, Maris, don't go off the deep end."

"But it's true. I have this . . . desire . . . this need, almost. . . . It's not the food, it's the hunting, the killing."

"Oh, Maris, really. . . ."

"I'm not a child," Maris said. "Please stop treating me like one."

His eyes darkened, bored into hers, and she felt uneasy. But when he looked away and licked his lips, Maris knew that it was fear that showed in his face. Fear of what? Surely he was not afraid of her?

"Please tell me — " she began again, but the children came running back, rosy-cheeked, excited, proffering wildflowers. Derek had no trouble changing moods. He smiled, teased them, threw Vicky into the air. It took Maris longer to recover. She repacked the picnic basket in silence. The sun went behind a cloud. "Let's go home," she said flatly. Adam and Vicky were too jubilant to notice how morose she was. They sang songs all the way home.

When they had gone to bed, she asked him again. "Are you ever going to take me out again?"

"Yes."

But he didn't say when.

If I had the choice, she thought, lying in bed at night, would I undo it all? Would I refuse the white wolf's bite? Would I have agreed to go back with Dottie? She felt ashamed that her answer was no.

She twisted and turned; sleep would not come. Thoughts shrieked at her. She could not give up what she knew now. And yet, what did she know? Nothing.

She looked at her watch. Ten past two. She would never get to sleep with this argument going on in her head. She needed to have it out with Derek. And if she still got no answers, at least a fight would use up this nervous energy. She got up and pulled on a T-shirt and shorts. The house was dark, all the lights turned out. But she was determined to confront him, even if he was in bed. Before she could lose courage, she went down the hall to his bedroom door and rapped. There was no answer. She waited and knocked again, this time harder. Nothing. She turned the knob and the door opened as she expected — no locks in this house. She didn't need a light to see that the room was empty, the bed still made, with the crocheted coverlet neatly folded at its end.

She stood for a moment, not daring to allow herself to jump to any conclusions. With thoughts held in her mind, like her breath in her chest, she went downstairs and looked in all the rooms. No one. The cars stood outside. But he was gone.

He had gone without her, out into the night forest, to run, to hunt. He had left her behind in spite of what he had promised. She felt abandoned, humiliated. What did she lack? What was wrong with her? No, it wasn't her fault. It was him. He had lied. She would not trust him again.

She sat down in the living room to wait. The minutes ticked by and she thought of how she had once thought she could love him. That was gone now. When he returned, he would face her anger, face his betrayal.

But immediately she lost heart and felt despair. She had no power over him. He could send her away with the snap of his fingers. He controlled her destiny completely.

And yet. If she knew more, about him, about herself. If he wouldn't give her the answers, maybe Barb would. Once she had planned to search the bedroom for proof of Barb's involvement with the Society for the Study of Lycanthropy. But Dottie's death had seemed to make it unnecessary.

There must be more. Barb had been involved; she would have notes. Hadn't she said she kept a journal faithfully until the TATT made her give it up?

The house was quiet, Derek gone, the children in bed, Agnes not there. She got a flashlight from the kitchen drawer and went back upstairs. In Derek's bedroom, she pulled the heavy drapes across the window. She switched on the flashlight and began to search.

There were few places to hide things in the rest of the house. Agnes had already uncovered the manila envelope easily, so casually stuck into a cooking pot. Maris had been through most cupboards in the course of everyday business: looking for pencils, lost toys, umbrellas, and boots. She felt sure nothing had been hidden in her room or the children's room. The bathroom was spartan and the sitting room too public. Obviously Barb would not hide anything in Derek's desk.

But the master bedroom had closets and dresser drawers, cupboards and chests. She quickly felt in all the drawers. Some were Derek's, others empty. Dottie Rice had been packing Barb's things before she died.

But Dottie had not done the closet. Barb's clothes were squashed into the small space along with Derek's. The top shelf held folded sweaters, stacked blue jeans, and rows of shoes. The ceiling slanted backward, so that it became lower deeper into the closet. Pushed under the roof were cardboard storage boxes. None of them looked like the boxes Dottie Rice had been using.

Maris crawled under the hanging garments and began to search. Most of the boxes held clothes, out of season or old. The smell of cedar chips wafted out. At the back was a box of baby clothes, tiny shirts and nighties no doubt worn by Adam and Vicky. She felt down inside, under the clothes, and touched a metal ring. Carefully, she pulled out a spiral notebook. In the beam of the flashlight, she could see the pages covered with Barb's handwriting. At the bottom of the box was another notebook and some pamphlets. She took those and hurriedly patted the clothes down and replaced the lid. She swept the closet floor with the light, to be sure no traces were left behind. She closed the closet, checked that the bedroom looked as it had before, and shut the bedroom door firmly. None too soon. There was stirring in the kitchen below. Momentarily, caution forgotten, her anger flared up again. She was tempted to rush downstairs to confront him. But she stopped herself. She tiptoed back into her room and pushed the notebooks under her mattress. Then she crawled into bed and lay still. Soon after, she heard his footsteps on the stairs, the sound of running water from the cistern. There was a wall between them, yet she could feel his presence everywhere, as if he could see through walls, read her mind.

She pressed her eyelids shut and forced herself to breathe deeply and regularly. Pretending to be asleep, she fell into uneasy dreams. The next thing she knew, it was morning.

CHAPTER TWENTY-NINE

"Why are you spying on me?" Derek asked her the next morning. He had sent the children into the garden. She was sitting across from him, wondering how long a person could survive on tomato juice.

"What?" She started guiltily, afraid to even think of Barb's journal upstairs under the mattress. She had not had a chance to read it. Adam and Vicky had pulled her out of bed. But he couldn't know about the notebook, she assured herself. "I don't know what you mean."

"You were in my room last night."

"I was not."

"I know you were."

"Did you see me?" she asked warily.

"No."

"Then what are you talking about?"

He smiled one of his now familiar smiles: full of cold comfort. "You forgot about the drapes."

Her face gave her away, she knew; the recognition on it was clear for him to see. But she wasn't going to be beaten yet. "All right. I was in there. I was looking for you. You went out without me."

"That's my business."

"But you promised to take me."

"I said I would, but I didn't say when. I don't like to be questioned. Or spied on."

"I'm sorry," she forced herself to say. "I didn't mean anything. . . . It's just that I felt hurt." That hurt was mixed with anger, but she didn't want to show him that.

He relaxed a little and even looked apologetic. "I keep my promises. Remember that."

The children were still in the garden. Playing with MacDuff again. She wished McDuff would run away. "What's the matter anyway?" she asked. "Is it something about me?"

"You should be more afraid, Maris. Afraid of what might happen."

"Between us?" she said bluntly.

He looked surprised. "I want to be sure I have not made a mistake with you."

"It's already done. There's no way to undo it."

"Yes, you're right. " He looked into the middle distance, his eyes unfocused, staring but not seeing into the garden. She wondered what he felt about MacDuff, if he ever wanted to break open the cage, capture the warm soft body between his jaws.

"It must be wholly your decision, you know."

"I'm not repulsed, if that's what you're worried about."

His face hardened. "I don't want another weak partner."

Partner. The word tingled on the edge of acknowledgment. "I thought I had already shown you I wasn't weak."

"That is yet to be completely proven."

"I killed the stoat."

"One doesn't have to be a hunter to do that."

Excitement stung her, went through her in shivers. "A sheep, then. I'll do it this time."

"Look after my children," he said dismissively. "I'll see you this evening."

It was not a day for Agnes. But in the afternoon, Maris heard a car coming along the lane to the house. A quick look out the front told her it was not Derek, or Mrs. Dunkley's old-fashioned Rover. A blue car that somehow looked menacing.

It was luck that the children were indoors with her. She made them crouch down in the sitting room, out of sight of the windows, and told them to keep very still. She cursed the unlocked front door and hoped whoever it was would be too polite to walk in.

Maris's heart thudded when the knocking came. She crouched with the children and held her breath. The knocks stopped and she let out a sigh, only to suck it in again when footsteps crunched their way around the house to the back. Had they closed the kitchen door? Was something left on the stove?

There was another set of sharp knocks at the kitchen door. Then the footsteps went off, probably around the other side. At last there was the sound of an engine starting up, and the noise of the car faded away.

"Why'd we have to hide?" Vicky asked, looking put out in spite of the fact that she had cooperated.

"It was somebody I didn't want to see."

"Why not just tell him to go away, then?" Vicky persisted.

"He might not have gone. He might have made me go away with him."

"Why?"

"Shut up, Vicky," Adam said. "Can't you see it's like Janice?"

Maris had been creeping up to the windows to be sure no one was outside. She swung around. "Who's Janice?"

Adam looked abashed. "Nobody."

She took him by the arms. "Tell me."

"Just some person."

She resisted the urge to shake the lights out of him.

"Why is she like me? Come on, Adam, it's important."

Vicky's nose was turning red, which meant she was going to cry. "Our old scabby nurse," she cried.

"What happened with her?"

"She had to go away," Adam said soberly. "She left us a note saying that her friend had come and got her and took her off."

"Daddy said don't gossip about it," Vicky said, punching Adam on the arm.

"You're not gossiping," Maris said. "Anyway, I'll keep it a secret. Promise."

This seemed to make them feel better. "Mummy didn't like her much," Adam offered.

"She was glad when she'd gone," Vicky said.

"Was she like Agnes, old and grumpy?"

Vicky looked shocked. "Oh, no, she was beautiful."

"What?"

"Like you, sort of," Adam said.

"All right. It's our secret," Maris said. She told them to get some cookies and go up to the bedroom for a nap.

"But we don't take naps anymore," Adam said.

"It's very hot today. At least lie down in your room. Have some quiet time."

"MacDuff's hot, too," Vicky said. "Can we bring him with us?"

"No!" Maris said sharply. Then, in a nicer tone, "I'm going to have quiet time, too. We'll lie down for an hour and then we'll have iced tea." To cajole them even more, she showed them how to make sun tea by putting tea bags in a bottle and standing it in the garden.

Maris got them settled and then went to her room, leaving the doors open so they could call to her if they wanted.

She pulled the spiral notebook out from under the mattress and began to read. The journal started in March, four months before Maris arrived.

. . . After this year's hiatus, I agreed to try again. I'm afraid not to. He might try to find someone else. D. says I can do it if I want to. He is never ill. To him it's survival. To me it's poison. . . .

. . . The society of loonies may be my only salvation. I need to talk to someone and the old ladies are the only ones who will listen. And they do have information, but some of it is so archaic, it's pathetic. Yet who else can I ask about this? I want to know, is there any way to undo it? Could I change Derek? And how will I ever know about the children? . . .

. . . I want to die. I can't die. Adam and Vicky need me. I thought it was bad before, but I didn't know how bad it could be. Am I cursed with this for life? . . .

Maris turned the pages. There were a lot of repetitions, but nothing about Janice. Maris flipped to the entries that began in July, when she had arrived in England, curious to see if Barb had written anything about her.

> . . . M. seems shy but nice. A little stuck on herself, self-conscious. I get the feeling from Mother that Mrs. Pelham is a bitch. Poor kid. Adam and Vicky like her which is saying something. They don't take to people. . . .

> . . . Not feeling exactly chipper but better now that M. is here. She's hopeless when it comes to housework and cooking but she amuses the kids and I can get a nap every afternoon. She's awed by D., what else is new? He scares the poor kid. . . .

> . . . Awful. Bad last night. I really tried for D. I swear he almost turned on me. He loses it sometimes when he's like that. He's no longer a man, just an animal. I couldn't help getting sick, could I? M. took the kids to Banfield. I'm so ashamed for all of us. M. was helpful

tonight. D. was a pig. He came to bed late, hostile and cold as only he can be. . . .

. . . I hate him. He likes to push and pull, it pleases him to torture me. Against my better judgment, I lost my temper. M. was terrified, I don't blame her. Derek better behave or she'll wonder what's going on. I don't want her to leave. . . .

. . . D. is overstepping the bounds, is he crazy? Trying to make me jealous with a little girl like her. He won't find anyone else to take my place. Who would do such things for him? No one; he found that out before. . . .

. . . I must make a decision. I can't live like this any longer . . . I know what he's planning, even if he thinks I don't. He went after her tonight. She acted like a typical teenager, staying out too late, but she's not a bad kid. I can't sit by and let D. abuse her. And he will. The memory of Janice still haunts me. God help me and forgive me, and forgive him. . . .

That was the last entry, written the day before Barb committed suicide. It was obvious that she had been depressed. *I can't live this way any longer.* Maris turned to the other notebook.

Many of the lined pages had been torn out. It looked as if the tearing had been done hastily; shreds still clung to the spirals.

This notebook was at least a year older than the previous journal, from what Maris could tell from Barb's references. The remaining pages were crammed with tiny writing, hard to read.

Barb had kept a section for her dreams in this notebook. They all seemed to have taken place during the last half of that year. In one of them a tramp lies huddled in a hollowed-out space beneath some bushes. He's dirty, looks greasy and wet, but closer inspection reveals the dark patches to be blood. His teeth are gnashed tightly together, cutting clear through his tongue, which sticks out between his lips, swollen and blue. In another a horse and rider move along the edge of a cliff. The horse suddenly rears, then plunges over the edge. Horse and rider crash to the rocks below. The horse lies upon the man, its back broken and legs splayed grotesquely. A pool of blood seeps out beneath the horse and reminds Barb of flower petals. Finally there is one in which a woman walks along a lonely path in a forest. Frightened, she keeps looking over her shoulder. She runs, trips, falls. Her mouth opens wide with silent screams before she dies. Maris thought it must be Barb herself in the dream, trying to run away from what she couldn't escape, couldn't talk about. Nightmares, Maris thought, and shuddered.

She was almost to the last page when the name Janice caught Maris's eye.

> . . . Tried to ring Janice again this morning. No answer. Tried afternoon, man picked up near teatime, said he heard she went north to Manchester. He had no real information. Certainly no telephone number for her. It's so frustrating that these girls seem to have no roots, no responsibilities. They think nothing of going off without a forwarding address. Well, she got away . . . and perhaps she will think us only mad. I know I must never let this happen again. . . .

Maris put the notebook down. The journal was pretty much proof that Barb had planned suicide. It was a good thing Mrs. Rice had never found it, since Barb blamed everything on Derek. Barb was jealous, too. She thought Derek was having an affair with the nurse called Janice. That's what probably drove Janice off, Barb throwing a fit about it. Barb was crazy. Crazy people are unreliable, Maris thought, then remembered those were her mother's words. Never mind, there were other more disturbing things to think about, like Barb's concern about the children being shapeshifters, and wondering if it could ever be undone. If you were once a shapeshifter, must you always be one? Could you do it of your own free will, or did it take over so that you no longer had control?

Barb had gone to the Society for the Study of Lycanthropy, hoping they could give her answers. Maris picked up the pamphlets that Barb had called archaic. They looked like reprints of ancient tracts on superstition: witches, werewolves, vampires, black cats. Here and there someone, probably Barb, had underlined the text:

Those that drinketh the blood of man are cursed.

Well, Maris had expected to see something like that. Old books were always talking about curses. She went on reading.

The mark of the wolfe may heal but its scar remains upon thy soul.

Uneasily, Maris ran her fingers over her knee. The scar was only faintly visible. But sometimes it itched. When she scratched, usually in the night and unaware of doing so, it turned red and hot, dotted with tiny pimples of blood. This was the thing that Mrs.

Dunkley had mentioned, saying there were no marks on the children. Yet. But would they need a mark of initiation if they had been born that way? That was the reason Mrs. Dunkley said they shouldn't leave their father or leave England. The idea that they might change bothered Maris. But the words that bothered her most were the next:

The werewolfe is evile, will kille for luste of the flesh, for the sake of killing, not hunger.

The knowledge of what she had become, what she now was, stayed with her almost every waking hour. Only rarely did she forget, laughing at some remark of Vicky's, feeling the warmth of the summer sun, and then it came crashing back.

Had Derek ever really said they would kill only for food? Or had she allowed herself to believe it because killing for hunger was easier to accept than killing for its own sake? She had not wanted to think of herself as a killer, yet she had lusted after it. Now the killing was as necessary as sating the hunger.

Killing was part of her. Whether Derek made her that way or had simply released what was already there, she could not know.

"Do it of your own free will," Derek had said. A trick, like Dracula making Jonathan Harker enter the castle of his own free will.

She put the notebooks away, started dinner, and welcomed Derek home. And when he said "Tonight," she put the sleeping powders into the children's cocoa and left with him eagerly, feeling the anticipation of the kill within her, like a goblin, gnawing to be free.

CHAPTER THIRTY

She watched him change and felt herself follow him in this metamorphosis. There was something intimate and passionate in sharing the change, in seeing each other's body shift from human into the shape of a wolf.

Then they were running through the forest, white wolf and gray, and it was as it had been before and yet not the same. More power, more speed, wilder and more beautiful. The gray wolf was keeping up with the white now, almost side by side, no longer so much slower or weaker.

The white wolf skirted the sheep meadow and went deeper into the forest. On the other side was a farm where there were ducks and geese.

Gray wolf sensed it was being made easy for her. The killing of a duck would be no more difficult than the killing of the stoat. Human hands could wring a duck's neck. Gray wolf moved off to the right, following the scent of new prey, intent on her own hunt tonight.

The dog lifted its head and listened for the sound that had awakened it. In the meadow, the sheep were quiet, undisturbed. The dog whined nervously. An old border collie, it would soon be retired. Accustomed to chasing minor nuisances, the dog did not like this new and peculiar business.

Gray wolf moved downwind. She sensed the dog and knew it would not recognize her as an adversary at first, but would whine and posture and try to understand why this creature that looked so familiar smelled so wrong.

Gray wolf moved cautiously. Her sights were set not on the dog's flock of sheep but on the stag that lay beyond the meadow. This noble animal would prove her worth. She would use cunning and courage and strength. Never could she be accused of being weak.

She walked carefully, on the soft front part of her paws, disturbing no twig, making no sound at all. She was aware that the white wolf had come up behind her. He would know about the dog, too, but the animal was no match for the two of them. The only danger it presented was the warning it might bark out to the stag.

The dog, for reasons of its own, did not bark. But the stag was not taken unawares. This powerful animal raised its great antlered head and then lowered it to face the gray wolf. Gray wolf did not falter but parried, moving in a circle around the stag. The stag watched with soulful eyes, twitching its black muzzle. Then it raised its head again, sensing new danger. At that moment, gray wolf attacked.

But out of nowhere came the dog, hurtling itself at the gray wolf, snarling and snatching at the fur and flesh on the wolf's brisket and shoulder.

Gray wolf was surprised for only a moment. She shook the dog off easily, never losing sight of her prey.

The stag ran and she followed. But then there were sounds behind her and she was distracted, and impatient not to be, but part of her pulled her away from the stag's hooves and made her turn at the sound of a creature's pain.

White wolf held the black and white collie in its jaws, shaking it ferociously. The dog's body trembled to a different rhythm, then fell limp, blood coursing from its throat, staining the wolf's fur red. Gray wolf whined, but white wolf shook the dog again and growled.

Then gray wolf heard another sound and bristled in warning. They must flee. People had stirred at the farm, alerted by the bleating of the frightened sheep. Someone was coming, thrashing through the brush. There were shouts.

White wolf dropped the dog. Gray wolf began to move away, back toward the direction of the copse. But white wolf stopped and turned.

A man was coming toward them, carrying a gun, probably the owner of the farm. White wolf bared his teeth; he was not afraid. His haunches lowered in preparation for a spring.

Behind, in the shadows, gray wolf was poised, her muzzle quivering in fear. Fear for white wolf, fear for the farmer, fear for herself. Deep within her, she had faltered. Gone was the exhilaration, the fiery assurance she had felt before. She was no longer certain of cunning or strength. What she wanted was to run back to the copse, to safety. To home.

Home. Gray wolf could think only the texture of the word, the grain of it, groped for the memory of it buried and confused between wolf and woman, and was suffused with loneliness for what had been, might have been, what might never exist at all.

Eyes glinting, breath harsh, the wolves waited, one pair of eyes riveted on the man and the gun, the other on her partner's coat shimmering in the now risen moon.

The farmer stepped out into the moonlight. They caught the pungency of his sudden fear as he stopped and stared. He made a sound like a sigh, a breathy whisper — "Aaaah" — and stood frozen, uncertain, lowering the gun rather than raising it, transfixed by some atavistic terror.

White wolf watched with deceptively gentle eyes. His haunches shivered, ready to charge. Gray wolf tore at white wolf's ruff, pulling him back. He fought, turned his head in an angry snarl, but she hung on.

"Mel! Mel?" Voices rang out across the meadow, into the woods. More people. More guns. Gray wolf now let herself howl a warning, threw it out to be heard by the men.

Coming to his senses, the farmer raised his gun and took aim.

He aimed at moonlight. The wolves were gone, silently, as if they had never been, leaving only the echo of a strangely human scream behind.

CHAPTER THIRTY-ONE

"You almost killed him," Maris said.

"A wolf almost killed him in self-defense."

"We weren't in danger. We could have slipped away."

"I didn't want to slip away."

"You wanted to kill him, didn't you? Just like you killed the poor dog."

"It was only a dog. Why go on about it? Would you rather it had killed me?"

"The poor thing couldn't have hurt you."

"Just like Barb! Crying over dogs and horses. Cared more for them than people. She'd weep over a dead horse and come home and laugh at sick jokes about an air crash."

"A lot of people do that. *That's* a defense, against being overwhelmed by it. People don't mean any harm."

She had been standing at the sink, washing, washing her hands; she almost couldn't stop herself.

"People hate us. They call us furtive and vicious, they accuse us of treachery and cowardice. They don't love us as they do their dogs. They wouldn't hesitate to kill us."

"But you're a person yourself. You talk as if you weren't."

His eyes flashed. "Perhaps I'm not. Perhaps you're not."

"But we change back." She reached for a towel and he took her hand.

"There may come a time when we cannot resume human shapes. When we will be trapped in our shifted selves forever."

Maris tore away. "No, I won't listen to that. I don't believe it. Tonight I felt I could change if I wanted to, go back to what I really am."

Derek grabbed her; his fingernails dug into her arms. "And what is it that you really are?"

Suddenly Derek's mouth was on hers, kissing her. She could feel his teeth, taste blood. For a moment she gave herself up to it, her mind strangely detached, curious to see what it was like, this thing she might once have thought she desired. Then she pushed him

away, prepared to defend herself against his advances.
But he laughed.

"You're not human anymore. Get used to it. And ask yourself if you're prepared to put this nonsense aside and face it squarely, all of it."

"What do you mean by 'all of it'? Killing dogs? Killing farmers?" Killing Janice? she thought suddenly.

His face changed. The lonely look was back, the look she remembered when she had felt more sympathetic. Tonight, when they returned, she had felt she would never be able to think of him without disgust.

"For a long time now, I've been searching for a partner. I had hoped Barbara would be that partner. It's not in my nature to act alone; it's not in the nature of wolves to act alone. Barbara could never give herself up to it and there were so few other choices." He smiled. "It's not easy to find someone both able and willing."

Did he want her to be his partner in senseless killing? Surely wolves, real wolves, did not do that.

He laughed ruefully. "You look horrified, Maris. Is the thought of spending the rest of your life here so terrible?"

She shook her head. Of course she wanted to stay! A month ago, the thought of never returning home would have made her heart leap with joy. But these were frightening terms. It meant no going back ever. Perhaps, in the deepest part of her soul, she had kept the possibility of going home as a safeguard. Had she ever been ready to give everything up forever?

"Be careful what you wish for; you might get it." Mrs. Li said that. So did her mother. But Maris hadn't wished for this. Not exactly.

"Forgive me, I'm tired," Derek said abruptly, and left her standing in the kitchen. She could hear him going upstairs and moving around up there. She waited a long time before she had the courage to go up herself and slip past his bedroom door. She was worried about the children now, guilty because she hadn't given them a thought since she and Derek had returned to the house. But they were sleeping quietly.

So many things bothered her, worried her. Derek's words were going around and around in her head. She felt certain her choices were becoming more and more narrow, that there were no longer options, that Derek was closing the circle and eventually he would be the only option she had. And if she refused, if she fought back, would he kill her?

Barb had written about that. *He almost turned on me. He's not a man, he's an animal.* Barb had been afraid of him.

Maris lay awake on her bed, staring at the ceiling, blinking back the images of the last few hours. And then, pushing them away, thinking of the future and what it would mean. What kind of a future was there going to be, wherever she was? She knew so little of herself now. She drifted toward sleep thinking that Barb had escaped. Barb *had* escaped. But at what cost?

Maris sat up.

On the morning of the suicide, Derek told them not to disturb Barb. He had dawdled at the market, taking his time over tea, letting the children buy candy. And instead of going upstairs to check on his sick wife when they returned to the house, Derek stowed the groceries and made lunch, things he ordinarily never did. If Maris had not suggested she go up herself, how long would he have waited? Perhaps he had wanted to put off the discovery as long as possible.

Barb's torn wrists. Maris tried to imagine Barb tearing out her own flesh. Barb had always been sickened by such things.

A letter in Barb's handwriting had been used as evidence of a suicide note at the inquest. But what had it really said except that Barb was tired and unhappy?

A horse and rider. Dead horse, dead rider. A woman in the woods, running afraid. A tramp covered in blood.

Janice might be living in Manchester, or she might be the woman Barb saw lying dead in the woods. Had Derek tried to make Janice his partner and had he killed her when she tried to escape? What was real, what were dreams?

He will kill me, Maris thought. Whether I do what he wishes or whether I don't, in some way I will be killed, in body or in spirit.

A few hours later, she awoke with a start. Someone was outside her door. She got up quickly, thinking of the children. Their door was open and watery moonlight came through the diamond-pane windows, bathing the children in silver. Derek was standing over them.

"What are you doing?" she asked in alarm.

He turned to look at her and in that light, in that posture, he looked like a hunchbacked beast with glinting eyes.

"Just looking at my children," he said.

"Are they all right?" She was afraid they had died, poisoned from the sleeping powder.

"They are well. And no doubt someday may be as we are." He took her hand and led her back to her room. "You look upset, Maris. Is something wrong?"

Yes, something. She had been afraid, for a moment, that he was going to harm the children. For that fleeting moment in the silver light, the idea that he might kill them had seemed real.

"I was just worried. I thought the kids were ill or something."

"Some might call it an illness."

"You mean the children? But you don't really know about them, do you? You can't be sure. And anyway, couldn't it be cured?"

He laughed softly. "Not a chance of that. Not in a million years."

He put his hand on her throat, but then he only pushed her back into her room.

"What a nice little family we make. Good night, Maris."

Be careful what you wish for; you might get it. *You might get it.* There must be a way to undo it. Mrs. Dunkley would know. Or she could call the society in Yorkshire and go there if she had to. Someone would know. Someone must know.

It had seemed a canny thing, a mystery for the few, a wonderful power. But it was nothing more than a dark secret, a shameful thing to keep hidden in a cellar. What would become of them? A family of monsters. A ludicrous kind of horror.

CHAPTER THIRTY-TWO

She awoke to arguing: Agnes's voice, unusually shrill, tempered by the lower resonances of two men.

"I said get off my property," Derek was saying, and in the background Agnes pleaded, "You'll get yourself in trouble like that, Mr. Forrest."

"I'll only have to bring the police, sir." The third voice sounded reasonable, patient, firm in the knowledge that it would win in the end.

"Don't be daft. Don't do that," Agnes cried.

"My housekeeper is quite right. There's no need for all of this. I'll have the girl phone you as soon as she returns."

"I'd appreciate that, sir. But you know I'm obligated

to follow through with this?" a man's voice said reasonably.

"She's only away for a day or two." Derek sounded as reasonable himself.

There was the sound of a door closing. Footsteps. A car starting. Maris jumped out of bed and ran to look out of the children's bedroom window.

"What's up?" Adam asked. He and Vicky were sitting on their beds, wide-eyed.

"Dad told us we had to stay up here," Vicky complained.

Outside, a blue car was moving toward the lane. Mr. Reynolds from the embassy? Maris backed away from the window as the car disappeared.

"Can we get down now?" Adam asked.

"I suppose. . . ."

Agnes's voice rang out again. "You're mad, that's what you are."

The children ran downstairs and Agnes stopped yelling. But when Maris came into the kitchen, Agnes looked at her severely. "Just as I thought," she said, turning to Derek. "You lied to that man."

"This is none of your business." Derek, seemingly unperturbed, was finishing a cup of coffee at the sink.

Agnes glanced around to be sure the children had gone into the garden. "I have a suspicion what's going on here. I'm not a fool."

Fear curdled in Maris's stomach, but Derek simply

raised an eyebrow. "I have no idea what you're talking about."

"You and the young miss, here. It's not right. Things should be fixed up proper."

Maris let out a sigh of relief. Agnes was worried only about propriety. Like Dottie Rice, she thought they were sleeping together.

Derek put his cup into the sink and turned to the door. "I'll be home at the usual time, Maris." And then, as if in an afterthought, he turned to Agnes. "I wouldn't want you to compromise your principles. It might be best if you looked for another job."

Agnes huffed and was about to speak, but he closed the door and was gone.

"The nerve! He begs me to come back and now he gives me the sack. Well," she said, looking at Maris, "I've no intention of going. Not with innocent children in the picture."

Maris bristled. "I'm taking care of them."

"You? You need looking after more than they do. How can your mother let you carry on like this?"

"I'm not carrying on. All I'm doing is being an au pair until the end of the summer."

Agnes huffed. "Well, if I was her — your mother, I mean — I'd come over and take you back. I don't know what the world's coming to, but it isn't pretty. My God, with all that's going on in these parts, nobody is safe anymore."

What was the woman talking about? Maris tried to be casual as she filled the kettle. "Like a cup of tea?" she asked. "What's going on?"

"Sick things, done by sick people."

"Come on, Agnes."

"See for yourself!" She pulled a copy of the *Sun* out of her large cloth bag and thrust it toward Maris.

The newspaper was folded open to a story about animal killings. SHEEP DOG MAULED. The story reminded readers of previous killings of sheep. This was the first time a dog had been attacked. "He was a good dog," a farmer's wife was quoted saying. "Devil worshipers suspected," the article said. "Is human sacrifice next?" it asked.

Maris put the paper down. Her heart was thumping. "This newspaper always prints this garbage."

Agnes drew herself up. "It happens I had a word with Mrs. Archer herself. It was her husband saw the pack of wild dogs. Not ordinary dogs, mind you, because they hypnotized him so's he couldn't move a muscle. That's how they got away without being shot. I don't like it, living so near to Branch Farm as I do."

"I didn't know you lived — " Maris said, and caught her tongue. "Nobody believes that junk."

"They do around here! And you should know; from what I hear of the States, they have plenty of trouble like that, what with child abusers, serial killers, and such."

"People do that stuff, not wild dogs." Maris threw the paper down. The teakettle was screeching steam. "It has nothing to do with us," she said.

"Who's going to look after those tots when you're gone?" Agnes asked. "Mr. Forrest? He'll get some other young girl like you and she'll have to go home or disappear and where will those children be? They have no one."

"I thought there were relatives in Selbridge."

Agnes snorted. "Some old cousins in their dotage. Not fit to bring up children. They'll have to be sent into care, poor little tykes."

"Mr. Forrest won't allow that."

"It's not for him to decide. It's for the council to see the proper thing is done. I've a mind to have a word with the district nurse myself and suggest she pay a visit. And I should think the council will send you back home as well."

"You have no right to interefere!"

"I'll thank you not to tell me my duty," Agnes said. "Little snip like you."

Maris felt torn. It might be better if the kids were sent away. Maybe they'd never have to know what their father really was. But what if this council found out the truth? What would they do to them all? It had to be kept a secret. A very dark, private secret.

The day dragged. Agnes went around doing her duty in the house, and for that Maris was grateful. She mopped floors, washed clothes, ironed. She looked around at her work with a grim smile. "I'll be off, then. Tell him if he wants to let me go, he'll have to do it right. Proper notice and all. Otherwise, I'll be back."

Agnes left the newspaper behind. When Derek came home, Maris showed the story to him and told him what Agnes had threatened. She expected him to be upset, but he wasn't. Instead he became jolly with the children and told Maris that he would make the dinner; she could put her feet up and relax.

"But what if she says something to this council, whatever it is, about me? And what about the children being taken away?"

"Not to worry," he said lightly, and got out pans and eggs and cheese for an omelet. "How about picking some herbs out of the garden for this?"

Omelets, food, she wasn't interested. The juxtaposition of such mundane household tasks with the stark truth was absurd. She felt as if she were acting in a black comedy that was going from ridiculous to worse, that could only end with disaster.

But it wasn't until he brought her the tea that she came to her senses. If any suspicion had been nagging in the back of her mind, she had ignored it until that moment.

She was in the sitting room with the children, watching television, and he brought in a tray, with the children's cocoa and a mug of tea for her. She looked at the cocoa and at Derek, but his face was unreadable.

Is this . . . ? she tried to ask him without words, but he gave no acknowledgment.

The children clamored for chocolate biscuits.

"I'll get them," Maris said, thinking she could pour the tea down the sink, but Derek said, "No, I'll go," and rushed out. Careful not to let the children see, she poured some of the tea into one of the flower pots. And then she pretended to sip until she could finally collect the dirty cups and tray and take them into the kitchen, protesting Derek's help with, "No, no, you've done so much tonight."

If he had put a sleeping powder in her tea, she would be getting sleepy now. So she said she would see the children to bed and probably go up herself. "Unless," she asked, "there are other plans for tonight?"

"No plans." She could read nothing in his face.

She went to her room, undressed, and got into bed. Downstairs, the television played, but there was no way of knowing if he was in the room or not. She stayed as she was and let an hour pass. And then she heard the television switched off and his footsteps on the stairs. He came down the hall to the children's room, opened the door, and must have looked in. Then slowly and quietly her own door opened. Maris forced her breath into an even rhythm. His shadow crept over her, made the dark under her eyelids darker. She stifled the urge to run and hoped her body would not betray her. Inside, she was trembling. Would he kill her? Would he lift her arm and sink his teeth into her wrist and make it look as if she had done it herself? She was sure he had done that to Barb.

She almost rose up screaming when she felt him bend closer. But he must have only wanted to be sure she was sleeping because suddenly the light under her eyelids changed and she knew he was gone. A few moments later, she heard the door softly open and close as Derek went out.

How could he be so transparent? she thought with disgust. He should have known better since it was he who had given her the sharpened senses, the cunning, the mind and heart of a wolf.

CHAPTER THIRTY-THREE

Gray wolf ran. She had to follow the fields and go through the woods, using the old right-of-way paths that snaked through most properties. If she had to use the road, she was watchful for cars and slunk under the hedgerows if one came along.

She ran to where she knew white wolf would be. In her mind she struggled to keep human thoughts and wolf thoughts separate, to force herself to keep remembering why she was running and what she was hunting.

She was hunting him. He was going to Agnes's cottage and he would hurt her, kill her, silence her forever.

She skirted the place where the sheep dog had guarded its flock and followed the scent of white wolf across a stream, over a hill, and down into a fold between that hill and the next, where a row of stone cottages stood, each with its square patch of front garden and its crazy-paving path to the door.

Beyond was a village where lights had begun to make an orange glow against the billowing clouds. There was a sound of a church bell ringing, the calling of crows, and the chatter of swifts crisscrossing the sky like bats.

There white wolf stood, ears pricked, body tensed, surveying the cottages craftily. Gray wolf stalked him soundlessly, her eyes watchful, waiting for some signal to tell her which was the woman's cottage.

But white wolf turned sharply, lip curled, a warning, menacing growl in his throat. He lunged at gray wolf, checked and pulled away. He crouched and growled, ready to lunge again. Gray wolf recognized these signals of intimidation. She cowered and mewled softly and began to groom herself. Satisfied, white wolf turned back to the cottages. A woman was standing in the doorway of the third cottage, her hand held over her eyes to shield them from the setting sun. Gray wolf immediately sensed white wolf's intent. And she knew she was not strong enough to stop him.

For the second time, gray wolf raised her voice in warning, a long throaty howl that sent the woman back into the cottage. The slamming door echoed across the open ground. The air quivered in sudden silence. From a distance came the report of a gun.

White wolf turned back, blind with fury, raging at gray wolf, at the world around him. His heart was wild, his soul inhuman. The blood and flesh of a recent kill congealed on his jaws. Gray wolf understood. She, too, had stopped in her pursuit to worry a rabbit, finding pleasure in cracking its neck between her strong jaws, swallowing warm salty blood. But this was different. The pursuit of Agnes was not hunting. It was murder. And although white wolf might think he was acting only for his survival, gray wolf knew there was a great hatred in his heart.

White wolf stopped for a moment. His yellow eyes looked deeply into the eyes of gray wolf. And then it seemed as if he tore himself loose from her, running into the blood-red blaze of the sun that set so slowly in English summer.

Gray wolf raced after him. They were together as they had been for thousands of years before, racing across a vast steppe, their valiant hearts drumming with the same memories, the same desires. The wolves, whom some mistakenly recalled later as large dogs, moved in contrapuntal rhythm across the sheep meadow and into the woods.

White wolf stopped short. In front of him stood a man, a faintly familiar man, the farmer they had met before. The farmer was no longer hypnotized. He raised his gun.

"Got you now, you bugger," he said with relish.

White wolf bared his fangs, drew a bead on the farmer's neck and lowered his haunches, preparing to spring.

Behind, in the shadows, gray wolf was poised, her muzzle quivering in fear. Fear for the farmer, fear for herself. Gray wolf was also prepared. She launched herself toward white wolf at the moment the gun flashed and exploded.

Thundercrack snap in her head, explosion of a million stars piercing her with a million bright holes. Her ear shrieked and went deaf. The sounds of evening were muted into booming silence. The booming matched the pounding of her heart as it struggled between two worlds, two beings, two souls.

She was lying on something hard, her bare skin covered with harsh cloth. Although she was immobilized, strapped down, her body careened from side to side as it was also carried forward at great speed. She felt giddy and faint, but a covering on her mouth and nose poured cold impersonal breath into her and kept her from returning to that netherworld she had come from.

"Miss, miss," a voice hissed. "Miss, miss, can you hear me?"

Blood and bone clogged her throat. She could not reply.

I will forget, she thought. I won't remember anything. But, of course, she remembered it all.

E PILOGUE

The jet lifted off from Gatwick Airport. Below, the green patchwork of the English countryside diminished and tilted until clouds effaced the view.

I have known those places, Maris thought. The spaces between the trees, the scent of the soil, the call of the hunt in my heart.

The woman in the seat beside her, flashing gold bracelets and smelling of expensive perfume, asked, "Have a nice visit?" Maris felt herself grow tense.

She had become acutely sensitive to questions, even the most trivial. She forced herself to nod and smile. It was important to appear normal. She had learned that in the hospital. Put on a blank face and act stupid without sounding rude. But then, no one would ever suspect the truth. The suspicions of the police and doctors had been predictable: that she and Derek had done something improper and indecent. Whatever they imagined, it could never touch the truth. No one could imagine that.

The woman asked if she was going home, looking forward to school. For a moment, Maris could not formulate an answer. What were those things?

"Sure."

She would have to go to school. She would need to act ordinary, do ordinary things. But she would be different in a way no one could understand.

If she let herself think about it too long, a tremor began inside of her, like a steel spring of terror that might never stop. Right now she could still feel herself on the inside as well as the outside. She knew who Maris was. She could contain the wolf, although at moments she wanted to let it emerge. Like when they were questioning her, she could have wiped those imperious smirks off their faces. *You've been a bad girl, Maris,* they implied and she was tempted to show them how bad. *I could kill you,* she thought.

On the phone with her mother, she felt like crying, at first. *Help me, make it better, make it go away,* she almost begged. But her mother's sympathy was short-lived and when she began to nag, Maris felt a surge of power. *You can't do anything to me anymore,* she wanted to scream.

But she shivered now, remembering. She didn't want to be like Derek. She dreaded facing them: her mother, Sophie, Ms. Epstein. They would all want to know what happened and she would have to make up something. Questions. People picking at her thoughts, pushing at her heart, probing her soul. In her luggage was the Chinese ball that Mrs. Li had given her, a good-luck charm, for strength. It seemed such a long time ago. Everything had changed, but only Maris knew it. The rest of them would be the same, and they would expect the same from her. It would be like trying to live in a picture book. What if she forgot and made a mistake? What if she couldn't control the wolf inside her? It wasn't a matter of killing others. She had to worry about them killing her.

She would have to find her way in this wilderness alone. She could ask no one. She could tell no one. This secret was not for sharing. The only people she knew who might possibly understand were two little kids in England, and she wasn't really sure about them. She felt bad about leaving, sorry they had to be put in a home, but she couldn't worry about it now. She was too busy wondering how she was going to live two lives in the same body, how she was going to keep pretending she was only Maris Pelham when the gray wolf was alive inside her. She had to appear weak and ordinary, when inside she was fierce, strong, and cunning, perhaps even vicious. There might be times when she would let the gray wolf out, when it would be necessary to do so. But always carefully, always with the utmost secrecy. She must never be found out.

There was only the faintest hope in her heart that somewhere, in America, there was another like herself. Now she understood why Derek had so desperately wanted a partner. The real terror was the loneliness, going on and on forever.